Death in the Berwyns

JJ Sullivan

Book 1 in the Claire Tanner Series

ISBN 978-1-910194-37-9

Cover designed by Jessica Bell Design

Proofread by Sharon Gray, Clued Up Editing

This book is a work of fiction. Names, characters, places, and incidents either are products of the author's imagination or are used fictitiously. Any resemblance to actual persons, living or dead, events, or locales is entirely coincidental.

OTHER BOOKS BY THIS AUTHOR

The Batterton Police Procedural Series

Drawn to Murder

Death to Order

Death Under Surveillance

As John Lynch (Contemporary Fiction)

The Making of Billy McErlane
    (first published as *Zappa's Mam's a Slapper*)

Sharon Wright: Butterfly

Darkness Comes

As RJ Lynch (Historical Fiction)

The James Blakiston Series:

A Just and Upright Man

Poor Law

Prologue

1990

She'd expected more violence. More blood. In fact, the killing had been almost surgical. She said, 'Where did you learn to do that?'

'Commandos. I joined up in 1939. Why not? There wasn't a lot going on here. The army didn't offer much in the way of pay, but they gave us somewhere to live and something to do and they fed us. Then in 1940 they wanted volunteers for what they called hazardous operations. It sounded good; I went for it and they took me. Taught me to live off the land, stay out of sight and kill Germans. 1945 – peace all round – I wanted to stay on but they said the army preferred people who'd take orders. Which wasn't me.'

'She didn't suffer at all. I don't think she even knew she was dying.'

'I hope I'm not hearing disappointment? You paid me to knock her off. Terrifying the victim costs extra.' He took a saw out of the bag he carried. 'I'm going to take the head off now. You sure you want to stick around?'

She shuddered, but she knew she had to make sure everything she'd paid for was done. 'I won't watch.'

As he went to work with the saw, she stared out of the window of the derelict barn. 'Where will you dump the head?'

'It will never be found. Anything else, you don't need to know.'

She'd said she wouldn't watch, but she couldn't help herself. Whoever had trained him had done an excellent job. 'The commandos taught you to do that?'

'Don't be ridiculous. We didn't behead corpses. You're behind enemy lines – you do what you went there to do and you get away as fast as possible. No, after the war the Co-op had this programme to help ex-servicemen. They took me on as an apprentice butcher. I got into trouble a couple of times outside work and in the end they let me go, but I was well taught.'

She checked through the woman's bag. Everything she needed was there. And now he was wrapping the severed head in newspaper. She tossed her own bag onto the ground. 'You'll make sure that doesn't burn with the body?'

He looked up – a craftsman annoyed when his skills were questioned. 'You'll get everything you paid for.' He left the barn and came back carrying a jerrycan, from which he began to soak the body in what she thought must be paraffin. 'You'd better stand well back. You don't want the smell of fire on you.'

A few minutes later the two of them stood on the hillside looking down at the barn. Inside, a blaze was well away. She said, 'The van is yours? You haven't stolen it? You're not going to be stopped by the police?'

'It's my van.'

'Good. Which way are you going?'

'I'll be heading toward Bala. More, you don't need to know.'

'Fine. You can drop me in Wrexham. I'll get the Chester train from there. Give me that overall.'

He took it off, handed it to her and put on the jacket lying in the van. They took one last look at the fire still blazing in the old barn, climbed into the van and drove away.

* * *

She took the overall he'd worn when he killed the woman and stuffed it into the back of a wardrobe. Jim wouldn't be back for hours and she needed to be long gone by then. She was tired and a taxi would have been good, but she didn't want anyone telling the police, when they started looking, that they'd driven a woman who looked like her to Chester station.

She dropped the key she'd used to let herself into the house down a drain some distance away. Four hours later, she got off the train at Euston and took a District Line train to Paddington. From there, it was a short trip to Heathrow. If you'd asked her, she'd have said she'd never fall asleep on the plane because of all the excitement she'd been through. She would have been wrong. And it was just as well, because at the end of this flight she was going to need all her wits about her.

CHAPTER 1

2022

Holly Evans sat back in her chair and eyed the almost naked young woman standing in front of her. 'That's very good, darling,' she said in an accent from which no amount of elocution lessons had been able to remove the final traces of an East European accent. 'And now the knickers, please.'

Without hesitation, the woman let the final garment in her striptease drop to the floor, standing upright and making no attempt to cover herself. Holly said, 'Nicely trimmed. You need to keep it that way, dear. Our clients are top-end and they are demanding. All right, one last step and you're on board. Think of this as an audition. We need to know you give yourself without reservation and with no sign of holding back. Perform to our satisfaction and this will be the last time you have sex without being paid.' She turned to the heavily built, shaven-headed man standing to her left. 'Laszlo?'

Laszlo stepped forward, took the woman by the hand and led her to the bed. She went with every sign of willingness.

Holly said, 'We need to see your full range, darling. Before he saddles up and rides into town, take him in your mouth. Make it look like nothing has ever given you so much pleasure.'

***

Claire Tanner held out her arms toward coach Jimmy Ojukwe so that he could unlace her gloves. Sweat was pouring from her. Jimmy said, 'Are you going through a bad time right now?'

'Bad time? No more than usual. Why do you ask?'

'This is a gym, Claire. People come here to work out. That applies to Mel as much as it does to you.'

'I'm sorry. Did I hit her a bit hard?'

'Claire, I'm seriously thinking about only matching you with men. You punch like them, after all. Okay. Go and have your shower. I'll look after Mel.'

Claire took her shower and dressed for work – suit, understated blouse, shoes she could run in if she needed to. The gym was only a five minute walk from Chester station and that's where she went first, though she wasn't about to catch a train. The area in which she had her office was not the sort of place tourists think of when they think of Chester. It wasn't close to the Grosvenor Hotel, the racecourse or the walks along the river, and nor was it inside the ancient walls.

In fact, a tourist would have to make a wrong turn even to stumble on Claire's office, because it was north of the station and the station is north of everything that makes Chester, Chester. If she was honest, the area she worked in was a dump. But it was all she could afford, so she made the best of it. And it did, because of the nearness of the station, have one thing going for it: the station had a branch of Costa Coffee accessible from the street as well as the platform. Claire had stopped on her way from the gym and bought a flat white and a blueberry muffin. She'd also bought a packet of cigarettes in WH Smith, despite promising both Jimmy and her mother that she'd give up.

She unlocked the door and took off her coat, but before she could start on her coffee and muffin the door opened again and a woman sat opposite Claire without waiting to be asked. Claire seethed. The woman said, 'Please. Get on with your breakfast. Do you mind if I smoke?'

'You can't smoke in here. It's against the law. We can both smoke out the back.' She took a long sip at her flat white. 'But before we do, tell me why you're here, so I can know I won't be wasting my time listening to you.'

That might be no way to speak to someone who could be a paying customer, but Claire wasn't sure she wanted a customer like this.

Flashy lipstick, too much eye make-up, two studs in each ear, which as far as Claire was concerned was one too many on each side, and a Gucci handbag that could not have been more fake if it tried. Private eyes get used to people with false fronts, but that doesn't mean they have to like them.

'My brother has spent the last thirty-two years in jail.'

Claire wasn't going to pretend surprise. She said, 'Before you tell me about your brother, tell me about you. What's your name?'

'I'm Mary Barnes. Barnes is my married name. I was born Mary Fitzgibbon, and the brother I'm here to talk about is Jim Fitzgibbon.'

'Okay, Mary Barnes. What did Jim do to earn that kind of time?'

'He was sentenced to life for the murder of his girlfriend.'

'Her name?'

'Sally Varney.'

'What was his tariff?'

'The judge said Jim should serve at least twenty-five years before he could be considered for parole.'

'So his tariff was up seven years ago. Why is he still inside? Why hasn't he been paroled?'

'They won't even consider letting him out until they think he shows remorse. And he doesn't.'

'I see. Well, that's bad news when it comes to parole. Most lifers manage to at least say they're sorry, just to get out. They don't have to mean it. Most of them don't.'

Mary Barnes shook her head. 'He's always denied killing Sally. He still does.'

Claire took a bite from her muffin. 'You haven't come to see me because you think I can persuade him to say he didn't mean to do it. So why are you here?'

Mary opened her bag and produced a sheet of paper. Claire found herself looking at a picture of a woman. 'Who is this?'

'Sally Varney.'

'You just told me she was murdered years ago.'

'The head had been removed and was never found. The body was burned so badly she couldn't be identified, but there were things with the body that satisfied the jury it was her. It wasn't – because I'm telling you, this is Sally Varney.'

Claire had finished her coffee and now she took the last bite from her muffin. She said, 'We can have that smoke now. But don't say anything about the case while we're outside, because it's a small backyard and we may be overheard.'

When they had both lit up, Mary Barnes looked around her in a way that compounded Claire's irritation. 'You're right,' she said. 'It isn't very big at all. Is that a measure of how big your business is?'

'You came to me, Mary Barnes. I didn't go to you, and I won't attempt to prevent you leaving and finding someone with bigger premises.'

The shadow that passed across Mary's face might have been remorse and might have been something completely different. Nevertheless, she apologised. 'I'm sorry. I'm upset. I know I don't always take other people's feelings into account. I came to you because you were recommended to me.'

'By whom?'

'Tina Howard.'

'Oh, I see. So you took this story to the press before you brought it to me.'

'Yes, I did. And before that, I took it to the police.'

'They weren't interested?'

'Couldn't have cared less. As far as they're concerned, they don't like the Fitzgibbons, they got their man, there's no need to go reopening cases and, anyway, it was all a long time ago.'

'We've had our nicotine fix,' said Claire. 'Let's go back inside.'

'Right,' said Claire when they were once again seated. 'You haven't been able to interest the police and you haven't been able to interest the press, so why should I let you interest me?'

'Don't you want to see justice done?'

'I'm sorry. I need more than that.' She picked up the printout. 'This looks like something off a social media page.'

Mary Barnes nodded.

'It says here this woman's name is Ellen Donovan.'

'I don't care what it says. That's Sally Varney.'

'And it says she lives on Vancouver Island with an artist called Miriam Donovan. Sister? Relative? Wife? It doesn't say.'

'She's Sally Varney.'

Claire spread her hands wide. 'And you want me to...to do what?'

'Go over there and bring her back. Or at least get her to confess who she is.'

Go to Canada. Claire would like that. But it would cost serious money. She said the last bit out loud. 'That would cost serious money. Is that likely to be a problem?'

'I don't have a lot. My husband runs the Moor's Head and he makes plenty, but he won't pay for this.'

'He thinks you're wrong?'

'He thinks it's all too late. He worries about how Jim would be if he ever did get out. My brother hasn't managed prison well.'

'Well…if you can't pay…'

'The police didn't ignore me entirely. They got in touch with the police in Canada, and they went and talked to the woman calling herself Ellen Donovan.'

'And she didn't admit anything?'

'She said she and this other woman had had a civil marriage ceremony and she'd taken her wife's name. She said she was born in Canada, she'd never heard of Sally Varney and she'd never been to England or lived in Chester. But I want her to have a DNA test.'

'And if she did? What would you compare it with?'

'She and Jim had a son. Tom. Jim's parents brought him up as their own. He thinks he's Jim's brother.'

'Okay, so half of his DNA came from Sally Varney. And if you got a close enough match with Ellen Donovan, Sally Varney and Ellen Donovan would be the same person. I understand why you want Ellen Donovan to take a DNA test. But what do you want me to do?'

'I want you to go to Canada and persuade her to give a sample.'

'Which, if she *is* who you think she is, she will refuse to do.'

'Then I want you to do whatever it is investigators do and prove who she really is.'

'Mary. You told me you don't have much money. I charge five hundred pounds a day, and I'd have to be gone for at least a week. That's three and a half thousand pounds. Then there's the airfare, the hotel bills, the cost of getting around – oh, and I do have this liking for breakfast, lunch and dinner.' She'd crossed the fingers on both hands when speaking the words 'five hundred pounds a day'. Chance would be a fine thing. If she made that in a week she celebrated with a treat.

'I can't afford anything like that.'

'Then, I'm sorry, but I'm afraid I can't help.'

'You're just like all the others.'

'If you mean I like to pay my bills as they fall due, I need a roof over my head and food on my table, you're right. I'm just like all the others. Thank you for the opportunity, but I'm going to have to pass.'

Mary took another picture from her bag and put it on the desk.

'What's this?'

'I had a picture of Sally Varney when she lived with Jim. I paid five hundred quid for someone to build a picture of what she would look like now. It's called forensic…'

'Thank you, I know what it's called.'

'Put it side by side with the social media picture. What do you see?'

'They do look a bit alike.'

'A bit alike? It's *her*!'

'Well, Mary, even if it is, and I'm far from convinced, I still won't go to Canada at my own expense. You must see how unreasonable that is.'

'What if I can get my brother to pay?'

'From prison? How is he going to do that?'

'I have another brother. His name is Barry.'

Claire weighed in her mind what she'd just been told. First, there'd been the mention of the Moor's Head, a notorious thieves' kitchen that told her everything she needed to know about Mary Barnes's husband. And now, Barry Fitzgibbon. She knew she'd need to be careful about what she got into, but all she said was, 'If he wants to put up the money, you can come back and see me and I'll think about it. No promises.' And she stood to indicate the conversation was over.

When Mary had gone, Claire locked the door behind her and turned the sign to say 'Back in Five'. Then she returned to the backyard and lit another cigarette. Of course, it would have been impossible to take the case. Apart from the lack of money, how did Mary Barnes think she recognised a photograph as someone she had known thirty years before?

People change in thirty years, often out of all recognition. And forensic facial reconstruction was by no means perfect.

Still, it would be good to know more about Ellen Donovan's childhood from people who knew her back then. And the son – Tom. Where was he now? How much did he know?

And then, of course, there was the overriding question. A body, headless and burned out of all recognition, was discovered more than thirty years ago. If it wasn't Sally Varney – who was it?

CHAPTER 2

'Claire? Claire! Don't pretend you're not there – I can smell the cigarette smoke.'

Claire stubbed out her cigarette, went back into her office, flicked over the sign to 'Open' and unlocked the door. 'I just had a woman called Mary Barnes here. She said she'd been recommended. By you.'

Tina Howard was a short, slim woman just the far side of fifty, with an infectious smile. She said, 'How would you ever survive if I didn't send business your way?'

'Any more customers like Mary Barnes and I'll be bankrupt. She has no money.'

'Her husband has money and so has her brother. The crooked one, not the one they've had banged up for the last thirty years.'

'She says her husband doesn't want to know.'

'One of them will cough up, don't you worry about that. Mary is an irresistible force.'

'I resisted her. Why don't you sit down and tell me everything you know about her and her brother?'

'I was fresh out of university and in my first month with the paper when Jim Fitzgibbon went to jail.'

'You covered the story?'

'Don't be daft. I was still doing Women's Institute meetings. Carol concerts at old people's homes. Ted Hughes had the crime beat. But he talked about it. He talked about every case he covered. He thought he was some old-style Hollywood gumshoe. Even wore a fedora. This was Chester in the nineteen-nineties, remember. Ted must have been the only man in the city who wore a hat.'

'And what did he say about the Jim Fitzgibbon case?'

Tina Howard smiled. 'That's the point. That's why I sent Mary to you. Ted Hughes said Jim Fitzgibbon was innocent. Ted never said that about anyone. He didn't have much time for the integrity of the police. In fact, he thought they were all bent. But a British jury never got things wrong. That was an article of faith for Ted. And yet, in this case, he was sure Jim Fitzgibbon had been framed.'

'I see. Is he still at the paper?'

'He retired years ago. But he still lives in Chester.' She took a notebook from her bag, tore off a sheet and placed it on Claire's desk. 'I took the liberty of noting down his address for you.'

'Did you? You know, among your many virtues, I never counted a lust for justice.'

'Claire. I don't know whether Jim Fitzgibbon was framed or not, and I'm not certain I'd care even if I knew for sure that he had been. The Fitzgibbons are not a credit to this city. But if he is innocent, and if you prove it, that's going to be one of the biggest stories we've seen in years. And who are you going to give it to, if not your old friend who fed you the story in the first place? And looked after you fifteen years ago when you arrived with your spanking new journalism degree and all the street smarts of a two-year-old?' She stood up. 'When you go to see Ted Hughes, you'll find a bottle eases the conversation. Nothing special – there's no need to spend a lot. Famous Grouse is his favourite.'

When Tina had left, Claire pondered what she had learned. She remembered Ted Hughes. He had learned his trade before the days of online news, when print was still king and pulling the wool over people's eyes was harder than it is now. If Ted Hughes thought there was something doubtful about Fitzgibbon's conviction, it would be worth asking him why. Not, of course, until someone had agreed to pay her. She wasn't running a charity.

Nevertheless, she took out her shopping list and, under 'Kroll' (which was her way of saying kitchen roll) and 'Fr Fr' (fromage frais), she wrote, 'Famous Grouse'.

**

Ted Hughes, retired crime reporter, took the bottle of Famous Grouse and examined the label. 'This isn't a social call, then?'

'Can't I bring a gift to an old colleague?'

'Were we ever colleagues, Claire? Hadn't I retired before you arrived?' He led the way into the kitchen, where he got down two glasses from a cupboard and began to strip the covering from the whisky. 'Perhaps not quite. But that trouble you had – that was after my time. I heard all about it, of course.' He unscrewed the top.

'None for me, thanks, Ted.'

Ted replaced the cap on the bottle. 'That's a relief. It's too early in the day for me, too. How about a nice cup of tea?'

'A nice cup of tea would be lovely.'

Ted made tea in the old-fashioned way – no teabags. As he waited for it to mash, he put ginger snaps on the table. He sat opposite her at the blue Formica kitchen table that looked as though it had been around as long as he had. 'Now. Why don't you tell me what you want to know?'

Claire bit into a biscuit. 'Mmm. Lovely.'

'Marks and Spencer. They're gluten-free, but that isn't why I buy them. Allergies are new – my generation didn't have them. These are very simply the best ginger biccies on the market.' Having poured tea for both of them, he dunked a biscuit in his mug.

Claire said, 'Jim Fitzgibbon.'

'Ah, yes. Poor old Jim. Not the nicest person you ever met, and not the nicest family, but he was stitched up – no doubt about that.'

'Who by?'

'I've no idea. But, if you're here, I assume there's a new lead. If you were still a hack, you might just be following up an old case for a human interest story. You know the sort of thing – man jailed in the prime of his life, still there thirty years later, how is he doing, what does this say about us as a society? But you're not a hack, you're a private eye. The only way you have an interest is if someone is offering you money. And whoever that someone is, it isn't a newspaper.' He pulled toward him a tin of Gold Flake and a packet of roll-up papers. 'Stupid question, given that this is my house, but do you mind if I smoke?'

Claire took her pack of Marlboro and a lighter from her bag. 'Not as long as you return the compliment. Have one of these?'

Hughes's eyes lit up. 'Don't mind if I do. I should have stopped long ago, but you know how it is.' When Claire had lit his cigarette for him and he had taken his first pull, he said, 'Maybe I'll try the prune method.'

'Prune method?'

'You eat a whole bag of prunes every morning. And then you're afraid to smoke, in case you cough.' And he began to laugh, a long, wheezy laugh that revealed a whole lifetime on the weed. When he was calm again, he said, 'Jim Fitzgibbon. Would you mind telling me what's awakened your interest?'

'There are suggestions that the woman he is supposed to have killed is living in Canada.'

'Suggestions? How strong are these suggestions?'

'That depends on who you listen to. According to his sister, they are gospel.'

'Ah. His sister. Mary Barnes, but originally a Fitzgibbon. Sister not just of Jim Fitzgibbon but also of Barry Fitzgibbon. Married to Bob Barnes, landlord of the Moor's Head. A whole bunch of warning signals there, Claire.'

'Agreed. But I was trained by Harry Knowles, and you know what a stickler Harry was for following every conceivable lead.'

Ted Hughes's expression had softened at the mention of their old boss. 'Harry Knowles. Best editor I ever had. Best editor anyone ever had. I heard he took it very badly when you had your little trouble. If he could have saved you, he would have done. But you know how it is. The Chronicle is a small part of a large group and the most important people are the shareholders.'

'Yes,' said Claire, who had long ago had enough of being reminded of what keeping her 'little trouble' quiet had cost the shareholders.

'I was very lucky to have Harry as an editor. I know that. But what interests me right now is Jim Fitzgibbon, and you just told me you think he got a bum rap. And now I have his sister waving a photograph at me, of someone who is very much alive, and telling me that this is the woman Fitzgibbon is supposed to have killed.'

'Interesting. Enough to make me wish I was back in the game. But there was a body – no doubt about that. So somebody died. If it wasn't Sally Varney, who was it? Why did no-one come forward to say that a woman was missing?' He leaned forward and took another cigarette from Claire's packet. 'How would you feel about having some help with this? I'd stay in the background, I wouldn't want any credit and I wouldn't want any share in whatever you're going to be earning, but I'd love to be involved.'

Claire could not prevent herself from smiling. She was certain she hadn't a maternal bone in her body, but the eager-little-boy look on the craggy face of a man who must be close to eighty years old would have melted a sterner heart than hers. She said, 'I'd love to have you along, Ted. Why don't we start with you telling me everything you remember about the case? Starting when you first heard there was a body, and not finishing until Jim Fitzgibbon was taken down the stairs after sentencing. I think I've got enough Marlboros left for that.'

CHAPTER 3

The Moor's Head looked like one of the city's better pubs. The furniture was clean and well-looked-after; the tiled floor had been renewed only a year earlier; the walls were washed down daily. There was the customary back room to which admission was by invitation only, but what pub has no back room? A stranger could walk in and never suspect that anything untoward might ever go on there.

Bob was pushing cash into a bag ready to be taken to the bank. This was something Bob had been doing for years; before he married Mary Fitzgibbon and took over the Moor's Head licence, he had been a bookmaker. Bookmakers take in large amounts of cash, and so do publicans, and as long as deposits follow a regular pattern, banks see no reason to alert the police about possible indications of money laundering. At its most fundamental, the business of banking is no different from the business of bookmakers and pubs. Or drug dealing, human trafficking and loan-sharking, for that matter. It's about showing a profit. And causing unnecessary suspicion to fall on its customers is not a good way to do that.

Mary said, 'I went to see that woman. Claire Tanner.'

'Oh?'

'The private investigator.'

'Was that wise? Do we want an investigator sticking her nose into our business?' He picked up his bag of cash and waved it in her face. 'Hmm?'

'That money is your business, not mine. I want Jim out of jail before he dies there.'

'Mary. You never doubted that Jim did Sally in.'

'That was before…'

'Before you saw a photograph and decided that was her. I know that.'

'It is her.'

'And the Canadian police say it isn't. And they've met and talked to her, which is more than you've done. How did Sally Varney get to Canada?'

'That's what I want the investigator to find out.'

'And have you talked to Jim? Does he want to get out? Because, if he does, all he has to do is admit he killed his girlfriend and say how sorry he is. It would hardly be the first lie Jim ever told.'

'She wants three and a half thousand. Plus airfare and hotel bills.'

'So five thousand, give or take. To find out whether some woman in Canada is not who she says she is.'

'You can afford it.'

'It's not about whether I can afford it. It's about whether it's a total waste of money. And it's about inviting some woman who makes a living out of sniffing out lawbreakers to take a good hard look at your business. Which means also looking at my business. Which is not something I would want.'

***

Ted Hughes took a glass from a cupboard. 'If we are going to revisit the Sally Varney case, I think I need a Scotch after all. You want to change your mind?'

When Claire shook her head, he poured himself a healthy slug and picked up the ashtray and his cigarette-making materials. 'Let's go into the sitting room and sit soft.'

They sat in comfortable armchairs on either side of an unlit fire. Hughes sipped from his glass. His eyes were far away. He said, 'When it all blew up, it seemed open and shut. There was a body, without its head and burned way beyond any hope of recognition. Without the head, there was no hope of dental records telling us who she was, and DNA identification was in its infancy. But there was a handbag close to the body. All of this happened down in the Berwyns, so it was the Welsh police who investigated at first, sheepshaggers to a man if you believed Cedric

Walters, but they did a good job any time I saw them in action and Walters turned out to be as bent as a nine-bob note. And the handbag had Sally Varney's purse in it with a driving licence and a few other things so it wasn't long before they got Chester cops involved. Sally Varney was living with Jim Fitzgibbon at the time, and you only had to mention the Fitzgibbon name to the Chester police for them to start preparing charges. They went and knocked on Jim's door and asked to see Sally – and she wasn't there. Jim let on he was as surprised as they were, but a word from Jim Fitzgibbon didn't carry much weight, even with Cedric Walters on the case. They got a warrant and when they searched the house they found overalls stuck in the back of a wardrobe. "Hidden" was the word used in court. Forensics said the overalls had been worn by someone who'd stood very close to a fire, and mud on the legs matched the place where the body had been burned. And there was blood. Jim was charged within a day, even though they had no confession, and the police were patting themselves on the back at a quick solution and a villain put away. You'd have thought Jim Fitzgibbon was Al Capone.'

'Cedric Walters?'

'Oh, of course, he was before your time. At the time Sally Varney was killed – or, if you're right, at the time someone we thought was Sally Varney was killed – Walters had just made the move into CID. He made detective sergeant four years later and detective inspector a while after that. He was tipped for even bigger things. And then it all unravelled, and it turned out he'd been on the take from the beginning. He was sentenced to five years and served three of them. He was particularly close to the Fitzgibbons. But he couldn't help Jim.'

'But no-one knew that at the time?' Hughes shook his head. Claire went on, 'In any case, you didn't believe Jim Fitzgibbon was the killer.'

'I did at first. I mean, it wasn't hard to see him in that role. He had quite a record, did Jim. But his behaviour was all wrong. The evidence against him seemed watertight. So what does a man who's lived a life like that do when he's caught bang to rights?' He looked at Claire as though expecting an answer.

'I don't know, Jim. You're the one who spent all those years as a crime reporter. What *does* he do?'

'He coughs. He says, "Yes, I did it." And then the mitigation starts. All the things she did to provoke him before he finally lost his temper and lamped her. The sheer magnificence of his refusal to descend to her level. The signs of her mental illness. If you have the kind of associates Fitzgibbon had, you can put a score of people into the witness box to support your story. And, of course, she isn't there to put her side, because she's dead. Then he would do the contrition bit. There's no shortage of crooks Fitzgibbon would have known who could have rehearsed him in how to show contrition to the judge. And then, afterwards, when the verdict has come in but he hasn't been sentenced yet, he does the contrition thing all over again, this time to the social workers and psychiatrists who have to tell the judge whether he regrets what he did. That's what a man like Jim Fitzgibbon does, to get the shortest sentence, if he's guilty and he knows he's going down.'

'And Jim Fitzgibbon didn't do that?'

'Jim Fitzgibbon denied murdering Sally Varney from the very start. And he still denies it, all these years later, when denying it buys him nothing and prevents him from getting his freedom. So that rocked my certainty a little. And then you start looking at the evidence. And it was so pat. So perfect. The head had disappeared and, unless someone was planning to make brawn with it, the only reason for removing the head is to prevent the body from being identified. And yet, whoever had done that had left Sally Varney's handbag close to the body. Why remove the head and leave the bag? And then the overalls – why would anyone who'd burned a body and cut off the head keep the overalls he'd done it in in his house? It was just too good to be true. All right, you were never a crime reporter but you've been a private investigator for a while now. How often have you seen all the evidence exactly where the police need it to be and in just the form that will get them a quick conviction with no argument?'

Claire shook her head. 'Never.'

'Never. Which is a good job, because that's how you earn a fee. By digging out what doesn't seem to be there. Am I right?'

'You are. Be that as it may, Jim Fitzgibbon went to jail and he's still there.'

'Yes he did, and yes he is. And if you can change that, I've no doubt Tina Howard will give you a write-up in the Chronicle that will make you so famous you'll be beating clients away from your door. It *was* Tina who sent you here?'

'She gave me your address, and she told me about the Famous Grouse. And, before that, it was Tina who sent Mary Barnes to see me.'

'Well, I've said it once and I'll say it again. Anything I can do to help – you've got it.' His face bore that distant look that Claire had come to understand as meaning not that his mind had left the building, but that he was thinking. 'I don't suppose anyone's mentioned Bert Musk?'

'Bert Musk?'

'They haven't. Well, this might be a complete dead end. But when they first had Fitzgibbon locked up on remand, he kept telling the cops to talk to Bert Musk. Said Sally had become very pally with Bert, and he – Fitzgibbon – didn't think it was sex that attracted her.'

'So what was it?'

'I don't know. I tried to talk to Musk, but he just laughed at me. And I know for a fact the police didn't bother to ask him questions. They had the suspect they wanted and, as far as they were concerned, the case was closed. As, indeed, it proved to be.'

'So where is Musk now?'

Ted Hughes shook his head. 'I have no idea. It's probably a dead end, anyway – Fitzgibbon clutching at straws.'

Claire said, 'You've already mentioned the big question. If Sally Varney is still alive – who was the woman who was burned? And how did she die? And what happened to the head?'

Ted Hughes raised his glass in salute to Claire. 'Finding the head would be a triumph. I don't suppose there's any flesh left on it, wherever it's been for the last thirty years – but there are likely to be teeth, and teeth could be compared with Sally Varney's dental chart. Which, I can tell you, Jim Fitzgibbon's lawyer got a copy of. Just in case a head turned up. And you can bet your life he still has it. Apart from which, DNA profiling has come on leaps and bounds since Jim went down. And they've got DNA from teeth far older than thirty-two years. '

'Do you know who Fitzgibbon's lawyer was?'

'I can't remember. But Mary Barnes will know.'

And so, Claire set off for the Moor's Head to ask her. But when she got there, she found she was out of luck.

Chapter 4

Bob Barnes had taken care to cultivate a 'mine host' appearance of the sort people expected in a pub landlord. Calm, measured, always available and never flustered or impatient. It was a persona that was not in evidence when Claire knocked on the door of a pub that had not yet opened and was admitted by a cleaning lady. He said, 'No, I have no idea where my wife is.'

Claire handed him one of her cards. 'Would you mind asking her to call me when she gets in?'

'I might. I might not. Right now, I'd like you to go.'

'All right. But before I do, do you happen to know who Jim Fitzgibbon's lawyer was when he stood trial for murder?'

No trace of a reaction was visible on Barnes's face. He pointed toward the door. 'We aren't open yet. So, if you wouldn't mind?'

It felt like a dead end. Claire decided to use the time to do what she did not want to do but knew, sooner or later, she must. She made her way to the station and bought a ticket to Manchester. When she got there, she took the tram to Audenshaw.

She didn't like the place and wasn't going to pretend she did. Her mother had moved here after Claire's father died and Claire and her sister, Daisy, left home. There was no family connection to Audenshaw and nothing that might have attracted Claire's mother except for one thing – part of a Greater Manchester that housed every race and religion imaginable, Audenshaw at the time of the 2011 census had been 97% white. The next census was due in a little over a year and Claire did not expect that figure to have altered much. Claire's last man, born in Barbados and looking like it, had referred to Audenshaw as Honky Town. He had gone there with her only once and refused to visit again, which had suited Claire's mother because she refused to believe that Claire had let him move in with her for any reason other than to irritate her mother.

It hadn't been forgotten, because the first words she heard when her mother opened the door and peered over Claire's shoulder were, 'You haven't brought *him* with you?'

'Him?'

'HIM. Don't pretend you don't know who I mean.'

'You're talking about Winston.'

'I don't know how they had the nerve. Giving *that* name to a n...'

'Finish that word, Mother, and I promise you I'll leave right now and you'll never see me again.' She pushed past her mother and into the house, but she didn't sit down and she didn't take her coat off. 'Just tell me, please, what it was that was so urgent that you had to speak to me and you couldn't tell me on the phone.'

Her mother walked into the fussy sitting room and sat down. Claire was struck once more, as she had been increasingly often on the rare occasions she came here, by the deterioration in someone who was not, by current standards, particularly old. There was a twitch to the woman's eyes and mouth that wouldn't seem to go away. She knew what it was, of course – it was fear. The grim reaper had sent Claire's mother a warning note in the form of a persistent cough. She thought it was probably lung cancer. She might be right – but there was no way of knowing, because she refused to go anywhere near a hospital. Claire said, 'You should get a doctor to look at that.'

'I'm not seeing a doctor. They just find something wrong with you.'

'And if you don't go, you stay healthy?'

Her mother coughed again. Then she said, 'Can I have one of your cigarettes?'

'I thought you'd given up.'

'I told *you* to give up. While you still have time. But you haven't, have you? I can smell it on you.' She held out a hand and Claire gave her a cigarette and lit it for her. 'Marlboro! Only the best for you. I get by on Carltons.'

'Mother. Why am I here?'

Claire was appalled to see the coughing fit that the first drag sent her mother into, so all-consuming that her face turned bright red and tears were squeezed from her eyes. When she was back to what passed for normal, she said, 'It's Daisy.'

Fear grabbed at Claire. She'd spoken to her sister only a few days ago and Daisy had said nothing about any problems, but Claire had met the man Daisy was hanging out with and identified him from the start as bad news. 'What about her? What's happened?'

'Well, I don't know, because she doesn't visit me any more often than you do. But I heard from Mrs Morris. You remember Mrs Morris?'

Claire nodded. Oh yes, she remembered Mrs Morris. A one-woman neighbourhood watch in the street in which they had lived while Claire and Daisy were growing up and their father was still alive.

'Well, she rang me. She'd seen Daisy in Deansgate. And Daisy saw her, although she pretended not to and walked straight past.'

Claire couldn't blame Daisy for that. She'd walk past the woman herself if she set eyes on her. 'So...?'

'Mrs Morris said Daisy had a black eye. And a puffed lip, as though someone had punched her in the mouth.'

'Have you spoken to her?'

Her mother stubbed out her cigarette with a look of disgust. 'Of course I haven't spoken to her. What would be the use of that? She isn't going to tell me anything, is she?'

'You want me to speak to her.' It wasn't a question.

'Speak to her, yes. But also find out what's going on. Whether she wants to tell you or not.'

'You realise I'm going to have to do this on the phone?'

'I don't care how you do it...'

'So why couldn't you tell me the same way? Why did I have to give up all this time and come all this way for a simple conversation that could have been over in two minutes?'

'Oh, right. So taking an hour to visit your own mother is too much trouble for you? I should have known.'

At the door, Claire turned and threw her packet of Marlboro into her mother's lap. 'There are still a few in there. Try to make them last.'

'You will call Daisy?'

'Yes, Mother. I'll call Daisy.'

'And you'll let me know what you find out?'

'I'm not promising to go that far. Just take care, will you?'

As she waited for the tram, she stood as far from anyone else as she could and speed-dialled her sister. When she heard Daisy's voice, she said, 'Can you talk?'

'That isn't true,' said Daisy. 'You don't work for Microsoft and there isn't anything wrong with my computer.'

'So you can't talk,' said Claire. 'Call me as soon as you're able.' And she put the phone back into her pocket, and realised that it didn't matter that she'd given all the smokes she had to her mother because she was standing in a place, and would soon be riding in another, where smoking was forbidden. Perhaps she should treat her mother's condition as a warning. Perhaps she should stop smoking now while, as her mother said, there was still time. Perhaps she would.

But not right now.

She was almost back at Chester when her phone rang. Hoping it was Daisy calling to set her mind at rest, she grabbed it from her pocket, but the number on the screen was one the phone didn't recognise. 'Claire Tanner?'

'Claire speaking,' she said.

'This is Barry Fitzgibbon. I'd like to talk to you. Are you in your office?'

'No, Mr Fitzgibbon, I'm not. But I can be, in fifteen minutes from now.'

'I'll see you there.'

CHAPTER 5

When she reached her office, a BMW 6 Series was parked by the kerb. Claire would not have recommended that street as a parking place for a vehicle at that price level, but if the owner was who she thought he was going to be he presumably relied on being identified by people of a criminal turn of mind to protect both him and what belonged to him. When he saw her unlock her office door, he got out of the car. She turned to face him. 'Barry Fitzgibbon?'

He nodded. 'You said fifteen minutes.'

She shrugged. Was Barry Fitzgibbon the sort of man to whom it was worth explaining that she'd stopped to buy her second pack of cigarettes that day? Or explaining anything else, for that matter? She walked into the office; Fitzgibbon closed the door behind him and pressed down the catch that locked it. When she raised an interrogative eyebrow, he said, 'I have no idea what sort of hours your clients keep, but I don't want to be interrupted. You can charge me for the time I'm here, if you like.'

Claire sat down and gestured that he should do the same. 'How can I help you?'

'Why did you want to know the name of my brother's lawyer?'

'I'm sorry, Mr Fitzgibbon, I am afraid that is confidential client information.'

He stared as though he could not believe what he was hearing. 'Do you know who I am?'

'You're the brother of a man who has served thirty-two years for murder and is still there. Is there something else I should know?'

The way he moved on his chair suggested he was fighting back an urge to respond violently and the fight was not going too well. Claire opened her handbag and, under cover of taking out a notebook, wrapped her hand around the pepper spray she kept there. Fitzgibbon said, 'Perhaps I asked the wrong question. Do you know what I can have done to you?'

Claire took the pepper spray from her bag and held it where he could see it. 'Mr Fitzgibbon. I've had a hard day and I'm tired. I need something to eat; I also need a cigarette. Those needs are making me short-tempered – the need for nicotine rather more than the need for food. So why don't you tell me what you want?'

His eyes appraised her in a way that said there was an intelligent operator behind the aggressive front. A way that said he was assessing his options. At last, he smiled and said, 'I feel like I should go out and come in again. Look – and don't feel you have to answer unless you want to – I believe my sister, Mary, came to see you. I believe she told you some tale about Sally Varney, the woman my brother Jim murdered more than thirty years ago, being alive.'

Claire listened while taking care to allow no reaction to appear on her face.

'You don't want to answer. Fair enough. But Mary has disappeared.'

'Oh? Is that unusual?'

'She's gone off before for a day or two. She's married to Bob Barnes, and Bob wouldn't be everyone's choice of someone to come home to. But this is the first time she's done it after pocketing ten thousand quid of Bob's money.'

Despite herself, Claire felt a surge of interest. 'Bob's money?'

'Well, it was in Bob's keeping. And, whoever it belonged to, it wasn't Mary's. And whose money it is will soon matter, because Bob is going to have to account for it.'

'Have you any idea where she might have gone?'

'She didn't leave a note. She did take her passport with her.'

Her passport. She couldn't have…had she gone to Canada? Was she planning to call on Ellen Donovan and accuse her of being Sally Varney?

Fitzgibbon said, 'I can see something is going on in your head. Any chance you might tell me what it is?'

'Your sister wanted me to go to Canada for her.'

'You refused?'

'I told her how much it would cost her. She said she didn't have that kind of money and I assumed that was the end of the matter. But if she's taken her passport and ten thousand pounds...'

'Why wouldn't she have brought the money to you and asked you to go?'

Claire shrugged. 'She's your sister, not mine. If you don't know why she'd do something, how should I? I met her this morning for the first time.' She stood up. 'Look, I have to have a cigarette. I'm going into the backyard. You can either come with me or wait in your car till I'm finished – I'm not leaving you in here on your own.' She waved the pepper spray in her hand. 'But I'll have this with me. And you will need to stand a few yards away.'

For the first time, the hint of a smile touched Fitzgibbon's lips. 'You're safe enough – I've accepted that threats of violence don't impress you. But I don't like being around the smell of tobacco. I won't wait in the car – I'll go home. There's a couple of things I need to do. Will you be here tomorrow?'

'I can give you an hour from nine o'clock. We'll call it consulting time and it will cost you eighty pounds. In advance.'

Fitzgibbon took a wallet from his pocket, extracted four twenties and placed them on the desk. 'I'll see you then.'

When he'd gone, Claire tucked the money into her purse. It was odd how much better a cash influx could make you feel. She fought back the temptation to blow it on a meal out. After a smoke in the backyard, she set off for home. She had a thick piece of salmon defrosting in the fridge. That, some new potatoes smothered in butter, and a salad would be the sensible option. She would, though, stop off at Marks to see what kind of wine she felt like drinking.

After she'd eaten, Claire telephoned someone she always described to clients as 'a very good friend and contact', though in fact friendship had nothing to do with it. When she'd said what she wanted to know, the other person said, 'It will cost you.'

'I'd expect nothing else. When can you get me the information?'

'If she's already flown, I should know within the half hour. If she hasn't gone and doesn't go, I'll never find out. But that's just as good, isn't it? You want to know if she left the country and, if she has, you want to know where she's gone. Knowing that she's still here answers your question as clearly as knowing that she isn't. Am I right?'

'You're right.'

Then she rang Tina Howard. 'What can you tell me about Barry Fitzgibbon?'

'Nothing' was the answer to that, but at Tina's suggestion she rang Ted Hughes and asked the retired crime reporter the same question.

'Barry Fitzgibbon,' said Hughes. 'I take it this is the same matter as you brought the Famous Grouse about?'

'It is.'

'All right then. Barry Fitzgibbon. What can I tell you? Young guy – well, by my standards if not by yours. What will he be now? Good grief, I suppose he must be fifty. I always thought getting old would take more time than it has. The Fitzgibbons were never what you might call a decent, law-abiding family, but it was all small stuff. Burglaries. Robbery with menaces. Blackmailing bookmakers.'

'Mary's husband was a bookmaker before he became a publican.'

'Yes, I know, but when Barry's father was a young man there were so many laws surrounding bookies that any time they weren't at a live race meeting, they were illegal. They didn't have betting shops like we have now. And in the early days, when Barry was a young buck making a name for himself, he was a small-timer among small-timers. He had the gift of the gab and he was useful with his fists. The kind of man one crook might hire to resolve a dispute with another crook. But that was it. No-one expected him to achieve anything, any more than they expected his brother Jim to prosper. And then he went off to the bright lights of London, and when he came back he was loaded.'

'Do you know how he made it?'

'I never found out. And, believe me, I tried. Barry's riches are a mystery. But they exist. I take it you know he owns a car dealership? He paid cash for it. You may not also know that he has a rather nice house in a rather nice part of the Wirral; he paid cash for that, too. All that cash made him a person of interest to the police. Money laundering – you can imagine the sort of thing. And I do believe Mary's husband, who, after all, is Barry Fitzgibbon's brother-in-law, does a bit of money laundering himself. But, from everything I hear, Barry is now legit. Which I'd expect a man like Barry to find boring. Does that answer your question?'

'It does, Ted, and thank you. If I think of anything else...'

'Then you know where I am.'

The wine Claire had chosen was a white from the Rhône Valley that was partly white grenache and partly two other grapes she'd never heard of. She'd chosen it not for any reason of taste or preference but because it was on offer. Normally, she'd have made a bottle last two nights, but this was only twelve and a half percent alcohol and she allowed herself to finish it. She was on the last glass and her second after-dinner cigarette when the phone rang. Mary Barnes had flown from Manchester Airport to Amsterdam on KLM. She was booked on an onward flight to Vancouver.

'She flew business class,' said Claire next morning.

'Of course,' said Barry Fitzgibbon. 'With that kind of money behind her, why would she do anything else? I imagine you'll want to do the same.'

'Me? When your sister asked me to go to Canada, I turned her down. She's gone herself. Why would I be going?'

'To earn your four hundred pounds a day. Why else?'

'It's six hundred, actually.'

Fitzgibbon grinned. 'Yesterday, you said five.'

'And I'll settle for that. But don't try to knock me down.'

Fitzgibbon took a thick envelope from his inside pocket and placed it on the desk. 'Three thousand five hundred. If you stay longer than a week, call me and I'll transfer more. My secretary is booking your flights.'

'You have a secretary? What else does she do for you?'

Fitzgibbon ignored the question. 'She's also looking at hotels. She'll be here in about twenty minutes to discuss which one you want. Then she'll book it and we'll pay the bill direct from here.'

Claire turned the envelope over and over in her hands, but didn't open it. Thirty-five hundred pounds was more than she'd ever earned for a month's work, never mind a week – but there were still questions to be answered before she took it. 'Why? If Mary has gone to confront Ellen Donovan or Sally Varney or whoever the hell she is, why do you need me to do the same thing?'

'I don't. What you're going for is to watch Mary's back. Who knows who this Donovan woman is? Or what she is capable of doing?'

Claire sat back in her chair and stared at Fitzgibbon. His face was giving nothing away. Did he mean what he'd just said? Was this really about protecting his sister? Or was there something more to this? Something he knew and wasn't about to tell her? She said,

'The information about the flights is costing me fifty quid.'

'Tell me who got it for you and I'll pay them.'

'Not a chance, Mister Fitzgibbon. I was once a journalist. I never betray my sources.'

Fitzgibbon placed two twenties and a ten on the desk. He turned toward the door. 'Here's Marie now. I'll leave the pair of you to arrange the details. Call me when you're in your Vancouver Island hotel room and we'll discuss the next move.'

Chapter 6

Marie turned out not to be what Claire would have expected in someone prepared to be a secretary for Barry Fitzgibbon. In her forties, smartly dressed, with an expression that said 'People who mess with me come to regret it', and a voice that suggested a privileged background and an expensive school. Claire said, 'You're not from around here?'

'No. I suppose I'm not.'

'Where did you go to school?'

'Claire. That is not what we are here to discuss. And before you decide that irritating me would be a good idea, you might want to remember that I'm the one you'll be calling if things go wrong and you need help.'

'Is that likely? That things will go wrong?'

'I have no idea. But I do know that Mr Fitzgibbon is more worried about his sister than he is saying. Why, I don't know. Perhaps he knows things that he hasn't shared with either of us. Now. How soon will you be free to go?'

It was a good question. Did she want to go to Canada? Well, did that matter? When she'd accepted what was, for her, a large amount of money in return for going there, she'd made the question of her wishes irrelevant. But there were a couple of things she needed to arrange, and she'd be happiest if, before she left, she'd spoken to her sister. But Marie took her silence for acquiescence and said, 'There are no direct flights to Vancouver from Manchester. But I can get you on a KLM flight at 9.05 tomorrow morning. You'll have ninety minutes in Amsterdam, to connect, and you may need all of that – Schiphol is a very big airport. That will get you into Vancouver just after two in the afternoon, which is nine in the evening here. It's a long journey, but that's what happens when you want to travel all the way to the other side of North America.'

Claire nodded. She'd have some arrangements to make, but she had all afternoon for that.

'Good,' said Marie. 'I hoped you'd agree to that and so I've booked it.'

Then why, thought Claire, *did you bother asking me when I'd be able to go?* But she knew the answer – this was the sort of directness a man like Barry Fitzgibbon would expect. She took the printed-out boarding pass Marie held out.

Marie said, 'Your return is open. Get the job done early, come back early. Mr Fitzgibbon won't expect a refund of any of the fee. If you need to stay longer, just call me. I'll fix the hotel and put money in your account. You'll find ATMs work just fine in Canada – it's a civilised country – but you'll feel better if you have some dollars in your purse when you land. I got two hundred for you.'

Claire looked at the notes she'd been handed. 'Aren't they pretty? Nothing like American dollars.'

'No. Not worth the same amount, either, unfortunately. I think that's everything. I expect you have arrangements to make before you leave, so I'll get out of your hair.'

But before she could go, Claire's mobile rang and Claire said, 'I have to take this.' Marie nodded but did not get out of her chair.

'Daisy! You were seen in Deansgate. What happened? And don't tell me you walked into a door.'

'It's nothing, Claire. He apologised afterwards. He's a bit hot-tempered – that's all.'

'Daisy!' Claire felt uncomfortable, letting an outsider hear her conversation with her sister, but if she didn't speak to her now, when would she get another chance? 'They always say they're sorry afterwards. And they are – until they do it again. There's only one cure for an abusive relationship, and that is to leave it.' And then the phone went dead and when Claire tried to call Daisy back the ringtone continued until a voice said the person she was calling was not able to take the call at the moment, and would she like to leave a message? Thinking that there was little point, Claire put the phone down.

'Sister?' asked Marie.

Claire nodded.

'Well,' said Marie, 'you gave her the right advice. And I'm sure you know she'll only take it when she's ready. Enjoy your flight. And enjoy Vancouver Island. I know it's work, but there's a lot to see there. Make sure you get a little me time while you're gone.'

Claire had been introduced to Dewi Morgan, a Welshman even then in his middle years, when she was a journalist. Born in Hawarden in North Wales, Dewi worked for a bailiff, finding out where people had gone to when they would rather keep the information secret and extracting from them money they would rather not part with, all with such good humour and friendliness that very few cases ever came to blows – but, if they did, it was rarely Dewi who came off worst. As well as his work for the bailiff, he moonlighted for Ted Hughes and any other local journalist who needed to dig out buried information about someone. And now he freelanced for Claire when needed. She phoned him. 'Dewi. Do you have a moment? If you do, could you share it with me?'

'I was just going to get something to eat. At the Grosvenor Brasserie,' he added after a moment's reflection.

Claire smiled. Paying for himself, Dewi would never go near the Grosvenor. She knew that, and she knew that he knew she knew it. In any case, it was hardly the most expensive place in town. It wasn't even the most expensive eating option in the Grosvenor Hotel. And she was enjoying her best paid week ever. She said, 'Give me ten minutes and I'll see you there.'

She picked up the files she knew she'd need, extracted from each the master sheets with names and contact details, and tucked them into her handbag. There weren't many; she wasn't leaving behind a huge number of open cases.

* * *

Dewi Morgan, even in his seventh decade of life, still had a build that could instil fear, though he used it only as a last resort. He had seated himself at a table that gave him a view of both doors into the building as well as the window and the street outside. A glass of white wine stood in front of him and another at the place opposite. He had a notebook open to his right and a pen beside it. He said, 'I ordered a glass of Chablis for both of us.'

'I don't think I'd better, Dewi. I've a lot to do this afternoon.'

'That's okay – I'll drink yours.'

It seemed pointless to say that, by the time lunch was over, he would have had at least one more and buying a bottle would have been cheaper than ordering by the glass. A waiter was hovering and she said, 'Shall we get the ordering out of the way? Before we get down to business?'

She picked up the menu. Dewi, of course, had already had time to consult his. 'I'll have the scallops,' he told the waiter. 'And then the Welsh fillet.'

'Certainly, sir,' said the waiter. 'How would you like your steak?'

'Just knock the horns off,' said Dewi.

'Yes, sir. I'll tell the chef you want it rare.' He turned to Claire. 'And you, Miss Tanner?'

'I think the club salad, Jonathan. No starter.' She handed him her menu, he took Dewi's and left. It had neither escaped her attention nor surprised her that, while she had ordered from the brunch menu, Dewi's meal came from the pricier à la carte.

Dewi, despite himself, was looking impressed. 'I had no idea you were a regular here.'

'I'm not. But we used to use it when I was at the paper – you know, if we had someone who was easily impressed and we didn't want to blow the whole month's entertaining budget.'

'Someone like me, you mean?'

'And then there was Winston, of course. He liked it here, so we came quite often. His treat.'

'Oh, yes. Winston. It is all over between you two, is it?'

'To the best of my knowledge. Splitting up wasn't my idea.'

'And if he wanted to come back?'

Dewi had finished his glass of Chablis, and Claire passed hers across the table. Ignoring his question, she said, 'Shall we get down to business? Before your scallops arrive?'

By the time Dewi had added a fruit crumble and they had both had coffee (with a brandy in Dewi's case), Claire had very little change out of a hundred and twenty pounds. It could, she knew, have been a lot worse and, in return for only three hundred more, paid in cash, which she knew she could not set against tax because Dewi would not be declaring it, Dewi had agreed to attend to everything she had outstanding. Claire said, 'Here's a spare key to the office. I don't suppose you'll need it but, just in case...'

'Okay, girl, that's everything, business-wise. Anything personal outstanding?'

'Personal? Dewi, I...'

'Daisy?'

Claire, who had been about to leave, sat down again. 'What do you know about Daisy?'

'Not a hell of a lot. I know she's your sister, which buys her a lot of respect in my book. But her fellow – I know a certain amount about him.'

Claire looked round, about to order another coffee, and realised that it was nicotine she needed. She said, 'Outside.'

When they were there, she lit up. Dewi said, 'Filthy habit, girl.'

'Tell me everything you know about this man.'

She had to hand it to Dewi; three glasses of Chablis and a brandy in the middle of the day and still he seemed in total control of himself and his mind.

He said, 'Jayden Walsh. Enforcer for loan shark Elliott Devons and abusive boyfriend of Daisy Tanner. Did time twice as a juvenile, for acts of violence. His father was in and out of prison most of his life, and when he was out he used Jayden's mother as a punchbag. Which, no doubt, is where the son gets it from. He isn't going to change – but a warning could bring him under control, at least where Daisy is concerned. You want me to see to that?'

It was a tempting offer, but Claire's relationship with Daisy was fragile enough without that level of interference. She shook her head. 'I appreciate the offer, Dewi, but no thanks.'

'Well – any time you change your mind, you know where I am.'

'One other thing, though – what do you know about a man called Bert Musk?'

'Musk? Old-timer, isn't he? A good bit older than me, at any rate.'

'You're still going strong…'

'I haven't subjected my system to the abuse he has.'

Claire, who had just paid for the amount of food and alcohol Dewi had tucked away, smiled.

'In any case, it's a question of genes. My father is still alive at ninety-six – did I ever tell you that?'

Claire smiled again. 'Once or twice. I hope you are as lucky. I need you around.'

'When I first got going in Chester, thirty years ago, Bert Musk was a bit of a player. I ran into him from time to time. Me on one side and him on the other. He used to drink in that pub your client's sister married into. The Moor's Head. Mind, that was before Barnes took the place over – but it was always a crook's pub, that one. Sometimes, they'd use Musk as a doorman there.'

'I didn't think they were that particular about who they let in.'

'He wasn't there to keep out the villains. Law enforcement. And people like me. That was who he targeted. He'd scare most people who couldn't handle themselves.'

'But that didn't include you?'

'We had a trial of strength once or twice. Then he decided it was better to leave me alone. I'll tell you who else used to spend time there – that defrocked copper.'

'Cedric Walters?'

'That's him. He wasn't defrocked at the time, of course. Looking back, it's amazing he got away with it for so long. But that's how it goes sometimes.'

'Anyway. Back to Bert Musk. You said he was out of the game?'

'Dementia. He's in a care home now.'

'Do you know where?'

'Here. In Chester. You want me to take you there?'

Claire looked at her watch. When she was finished with Dewi, all she had to do was check in to the airport hotel in time for tomorrow's flight. And she'd learned when she first became a journalist that stories don't wait. Leave a lead till later and it might be gone. And let's be frank – a man ten years older than Dewi Morgan who was in a care home and suffering from dementia might be dead by the time she was done on Vancouver

Island and ready to fly home. 'Sure,' she said. 'Lead the way.'

'There's a taxi rank just along the road. I take it you'll pick up the bill.' It wasn't a question.

They were well received at the care home's reception desk. 'Mr Musk doesn't get many visitors. In fact, I can't remember the last.'

Claire said, 'Will he be able to talk to us?'

'I haven't seen him today. He has his good days. But he has his bad days, too.'

'In the old days,' muttered Dewi Morgan, 'those were the only kind he had.'

They followed the receptionist along the corridor. Claire said, 'Is this a private home?'

'No. But I promise you, our residents get the best possible care and treatment.' She knocked at a door, waited a respectful fifteen seconds and then looked inside. 'He isn't in his room. That's a good sign. We have several lounges here; let's go and find which one he's in.'

When they found him, Claire assumed that this must be a good day because Musk recognised Dewi Morgan. She wasn't sure that she had ever seen a look of such slyness on a human face. 'Mr Morgan. How nice of you to visit. You brought me anything?'

'A visitor, Bert. When did you last have one of those?'

'I'd have preferred a bottle of whisky. Who is she?'

Claire was about to answer, but Morgan got in first. 'A journalist, Bert. Works for one of the nationals. She wants to put you in the papers.'

Claire was conscious of being studied by an expert. If this was how it got you, dementia wasn't as bad as it was cracked up to be. The receptionist said, 'I'll leave you now. You can find your way out when you're done?'

Claire thanked her. Something else she'd learned early and was unlikely to forget was that people cooperated much more willingly when the memories they had of you were good. And how could she know whether she'd ever need to come here again? Musk had not taken his eyes from her. 'In the papers, eh? There'd be something in it for me, then?'

'I'm sure there will, Bert.'

Musk glanced at the two ancient residents sitting nearby, who were paying them close attention. He nodded toward the corner. 'Let's go over there, then. Where we can't be overheard.'

He had two sticks to walk with; even so, they each needed to take one arm. Claire's overwhelming impression was of frailty. When they were sitting again, he said, 'So what do you want to know?'

'What can you tell me about Sally Varney?'

Musk's silence went on for a considerable time, while his face registered – what? Claire wasn't sure. Contempt? Derision? What she was certain of was that he knew who Sally Varney was; he didn't even try to hide it.

'Dead,' Musk said. 'Murdered by Jim Fitzgibbon. He got life for it. You don't need me to tell you that.'

'Did you know her?'

'I'll say I did, if it's worth money.'

Claire took twenty pounds from her purse, folded it and held it in her hand.

'Okay, for twenty quid, I knew her. I didn't, but that won't bother a journalist, will it? I've had my name in the papers before, you know. Usually, I didn't like it.'

'What can you tell me about who killed her and why?'

Musk was looking bored. He said, 'The police said Jim Fitzgibbon killed her, and the jury agreed, so I suppose he must have done. Jim said he didn't, but he would say that, wouldn't he? And people didn't pay much heed to anything a Fitzgibbon said.'

'But what do you think?'

The smile on his face now was mocking. 'Me? How would I know? I wasn't there. Don't even know where it was done. As for why – well, Fitzgibbon wasn't the sanest person you ever met. If she got him mad enough, he might not have needed anything someone like you would call a reason. Do I get my twenty quid now?'

Claire held the note aloft between thumb and forefinger. 'Sure. In return for answering one question. Do you think Fitzgibbon murdered Sally Varney?'

Once again, Musk stared at her for some time. Then, 'No,' he said. 'If you want my honest opinion, I don't think he did.'

'In fact,' said Claire, 'do you think Sally Varney was murdered?'

The change in Musk's expression was immediate. He had looked like someone enjoying a bit of banter. Now, he looked like someone who wanted her to leave. He held out his hand. 'That was two questions.' When Claire had put the twenty-pound note into his hand, he said, 'Someone was murdered. Must have been. They couldn't have had a trial otherwise. Could they?'

'Yes,' said Claire, 'someone died. But was it Sally Varney?'

'I'm tired. Would you mind going now?'

'I'm going on a trip. To Canada. Can I come and see you again when I get back?'

'Best not. I get a bit overexcited. And if you did, I might be having one of my bad days. In fact, you can count on it.'

But Claire had noticed how he started when she said she was going to Canada, and she thought she'd got what she had come here for.

A train ticket from Chester to Manchester airport would cost her twenty-five pounds, against more than fifty for a taxi. But she planned to bill all of her expenses to Barry Fitzgibbon, and that included the room she had booked that night at Manchester Airport's Radisson Blu Hotel, and the dinner she intended to eat there. What's more, a taxi would take about forty minutes instead of eighty. A no-brainer. She spent the rest of the afternoon packing, and emptying her fridge of everything that might not survive seven days, before leaving home in a taxi just after five. Plenty of time for a relaxing meal, a soak in the bath, and an early night to prepare for her flight next day.

The only thing that went wrong with that plan was that the hotel room had a shower but no tub. No big deal – she found she was looking forward to this trip. And the meal, though typical hotel 'international' fare, was a break from cooking for herself.

She set the alarm on her smartphone for five the next morning, and it was just as well that she did because she slept like a baby.

CHAPTER 7

Holly Evans was halfway through what she called the onboarding of a new girl. A careful document check had shown she had been born in the UK and was twenty-one years old. Two things Holly was immovable on: she would find no work for illegals, or for anyone underage. The girl appeared to be clean, spoke nicely and seemed able to keep up an intelligent conversation. That mattered when your clients were paying serious money for someone to spend a night or a weekend with them in an upmarket hotel. Especially if they were acting as escorts at a conference or other meeting where they might be expected to interact with wives and girlfriends as well as the client. Still, there was one set of attributes that took precedence over all others.

She said, 'When you join us, you are joining the cream of the profession. No rooms where nobody knows where you are. No risks from drugged-up pimps. And nobody taking almost all the money you earn. Our clients pay you. They pay you in cash. So you know what's been paid for your services and you get to keep half of it. The other half you give to Laszlo here. We know the amount that was agreed, so you won't be tempted to cheat us and you'll be able to see that we aren't cheating you. A lot of clients tip the girls afterwards and those tips are yours to keep. You can do very well with us. The reason I'm hiring a new girl now is because one who joined us four years ago was doing a BA in fashion design. She's saved her client money and now she has enough to set up an online nightwear business. That's the kind of success we encourage. You won't get there if you use drugs or alcohol. If Laszlo gets the slightest hint when he delivers you to a client that you've been snorting, smoking or injecting anything, our relationship is terminated. Of course, you'll drink with the client, but moderation, please.

'Now. You need to be an actress to do well in this business. I want you to imagine you and the client have checked in to the kind of hotel that expects its guests to drop up to a thousand pounds on a room, dinner, wine and the other little odds and ends that make up a bill. You're back in your room after dinner and the client is looking for one more pleasure before the sleep he believes he has earned. That pleasure does not begin when he gets into bed; it starts before that. And your job is to provide it. Let me see how you reveal the offer. I want to see you oozing anticipation and enticement, even though the man you're about to give yourself to is sixty years old with a pot belly and hair growing out of his nose. Start by taking off your dress.'

Manchester to Amsterdam was a 737, and uneventful. It landed at Gate D12. The departure gate was right at the far end of the other D pier – a fifteen-minute walk – and so Claire didn't need the time Marie had said she might. She sat and did what journalists, private investigators and policemen usually do; she watched people. The aircraft, when the flight was called, was an Airbus 330 and Claire turned left at the door to find herself in a cabin with eighteen seats. A flight attendant led the way to a window seat in the back row, tucked Claire's cabin bag into an overhead locker and asked whether she would like a glass of champagne. It would, Claire thought, be silly not to say yes – and it was, after all, already afternoon in the Netherlands.

The seats in this cabin were arranged in pairs. A woman in her forties, quietly but expensively dressed, was shown to the seat next to Claire. Without sparing Claire a glance, she extracted a laptop from her cabin bag and dropped it into the large pocket on the back of the seat in front before allowing the bag to be stowed away. When they were in the air and the seat-belt signs had been switched off, she opened the laptop, switched it on and spent the next three hours, apart from a break to eat, examining spreadsheets. Then she put the laptop away, adjusted her seat so that it became almost flat and very like a bed, and drifted off to sleep. A member of cabin crew placed a blanket over her. At no point had the woman even acknowledged Claire's presence.

Nine hours after take-off, the steward who had brought her champagne stood before her again with a tray containing a number of blue and white houses of a kind common in Amsterdam. Claire raised an eyebrow. The steward said, 'You haven't flown with us before?' Claire shook her head. 'We have a whole range of these, and each business-class passenger can choose one at the end of each long-distance flight. We have long-time flyers who've collected the whole range. They are free,' he went on. 'And they contain gin.'

'Gin?'

'Except when we fly to places like Saudi Arabia. Then they are empty. Collectors don't generally drink the gin.' He smiled. 'But there's nothing to stop them if that's what they want to do.'

Claire looked over the collection on the tray and picked up a tall, narrow house of several stories with shutters open on the lower windows. The steward said, 'That's one of our earliest.' He handed her a booklet. 'We add new models all the time, but this is our latest range. It will help you choose the one you want on your next flight. Some regular passengers become so engaged that they find people to swap with so that they can complete their collection.'

The woman next to Claire picked up a house, checked the number on the bottom and put it down again. She did the same with three more houses before finding one she wanted. There was still not a word of communication with Claire.

Before long, there was a change in the aircraft's inclination, with the nose now a little lower than the tail. A while after that, the seat-belt lights came on again and the captain told them they had begun their descent. For the first time, Claire began to look out of the window to see what this country she was visiting was like. What struck her most, apart from the fact that it looked a lot like home, was the regular straightness of the roads. As they got lower, she could see that the cars were very like those she was familiar with, but the trucks were much, much larger. And they were all on the wrong side of the road.

And then they were very low indeed and the homes passing beneath them were arranged on a regular and orderly grid. And, finally, they were crossing what looked like a river channel and then the outskirts, of what might have been any airport, were speeding by below them and they were down, rolling at a rapidly reducing speed along a wide stretch of asphalt.

The moment the aircraft came to a stop, the woman in the next seat was out of it, retrieving her cabin bag and turning right toward the exit. Claire followed her example and, although she knew she shouldn't, felt an irresistible pleasure when she saw that the economy passengers were being held back until she and her fellow VIPs had disembarked. She followed the others to passport control, where she noticed that the woman who had sat beside her turned toward the desks for Canadian passport holders and was gone. Getting to the other side was slower for Claire because she had to answer questions about why she was there. Thinking it unwise to say that she was investigating a Canadian citizen, she said, 'I'm on holiday.'

'Enjoy your stay,' said the agent, and she was through. Baggage reclaim was busy and the woman she had sat beside was nowhere to be seen. Had she had everything she needed in that cabin bag? It would seem so. Claire retrieved her own checked bag and went outside to find a taxi to take her to the Horseshoe Bay ferry terminal for Vancouver Island.

Most of the ferry passengers appeared to be travelling by car or recreational vehicle, but she joined a number of other walk-on passengers. The crossing took less than two hours and although, by the time she had walked off the ferry, found a taxi and arrived at the Fairmont Empress, it was more than twenty hours since she had checked out of the Radisson Blu at Manchester Airport, she was so fascinated by this different world that she scarcely noticed. That changed when she reached her room and tiredness hit her like a punch. She sent a text to Marie saying 'Checked in. Going to take a nap', hung a 'Do not disturb' sign on the door, took off her clothes and slipped between the sheets of a king-size bed.

It was only when she woke four hours later that she looked from her window and saw that she had a view of the harbour. But this was not the harbour she had landed in from Vancouver. It couldn't have been, because the taxi ride had cost her two hundred and fifty bucks and she'd had to get the driver to stop at a bank so she could turn pounds into dollars. No wonder he had looked pleased when she told him where she was going. She hadn't understood how big Vancouver Island was until then. She would learn later that she could have flown in a seaplane from Vancouver direct to the stretch of water she was now looking at for half the price, but how could she have known?

* * *

It was midnight in Chester when Claire's text arrived, and Marie was alone and fast asleep. Barry Fitzgibbon and Bob Barnes, however, were still awake and neither was enjoying their conversation. Bob said, 'I have to make good that ten thousand quid by Friday or I'm in deep trouble.'

'I hear that,' said Barry. 'And I understand it. What I don't understand is why you think it's my business.'

'She's your sister.'

'And your wife. I think you'll find the law makes men responsible for their wives before it makes them responsible for their sisters.'

'The law? We're not talking about the law. It isn't the law that's going to come through that door on Friday night.'

'But it is the law that's going to give me a charge over whatever you're offering as security for a loan.'

'Security?'

'You were hoping for a gift?'

'I was hoping for a gentleman's agreement.'

Fitzgibbon made a show of looking around. 'Wouldn't that need two gentlemen? I don't see any in here. Bob, if you want ten thousand pounds out of me, you have to pay it back and you have to offer me something in return.'

'I expected better than that from you. For family reasons, if nothing else. I suppose I could give you a charge over this building.'

'Yes, you could, but I'd have to do a search to find out who comes before me.'

'Nobody. I own the pub, free and clear.'

'Do you? I had no idea business was so good. Perhaps I should come in as a partner.' When Barnes seemed about to object, Fitzgibbon said, 'It was a joke, Bob. I'd hate to be your business partner. I'd have to be on my guard all the time, looking for ways you were trying to cheat me. No – I've got a better idea. There's something I need and you can get it for me.'

When he told Barnes what he wanted, Barnes said, 'You can't be serious. I'm no burglar.'

'I know that, Bob. But there are burglars in and out of this place every day, now aren't there? And you know who they are.'

'But...'

'I'm not interested in buts, Bob. You deliver what I want by midday on Friday and I'll have ten thousand pounds waiting for you. And it won't be a loan, it will be payment for services rendered. Fail and you get nothing.' He patted Barnes on the shoulder. 'You're not going to get a better offer than that anywhere. Let's face it, any normal businessman who owned a pub like this with no mortgage could raise a ten thousand pound bank loan without the slightest difficulty. But you are not a normal businessman. Are you? Normal businessmen don't have a record for fraud.'

'That's rich, coming from you.'

'But I was never charged, Bob. It's a big difference.'

CHAPTER 8

Before leaving Chester, Claire had called the same person who had given her Mary Barnes's flight details and told him Mary's mobile phone number. She was just thinking about breakfast when a message came through on her smartphone. It was made up of GPS coordinates. She entered them into her phone's navigation app. That was something of a relief – wherever Mary was, it wasn't far from the Fairmont Empress. She replied to the message: This may be more difficult. There's a woman on social media called Ellen Donovan. All I know is that her partner is an artist called Miriam Donovan and she lives on Vancouver Island – but where?

Then she stood outside the hotel and smoked a cigarette, after which she went for breakfast and was astonished by how hungry she felt. During this meal she decided to stick to coffee while she was in Canada, because Canadians' idea of a cup of tea was not hers. She wondered whether to say that what they called 'English muffins' were no such thing, but decided they had probably been told that many times before. The eggs Benedict, however, were first rate.

The app on her phone said that the place where Mary was staying was close enough to walk. She set off, carrying some of the more recondite tools of the investigator's trade. Mary's hotel opened straight onto the street and, if those windows above the entrance were bedrooms, it would be a lot noisier than the Empress. She went to Reception, where a young woman smiled a welcome. Claire said, 'I believe you have a Mary Barnes staying here?'

The receptionist, smile still in place, consulted her computer terminal. 'That's right. We have. I can't give you her room number, but, if she's in, would you like to speak to her?' When Claire said she would, the receptionist dialled a number, waited for an answer and then handed the phone to Claire.

'Mary? Mary Barnes?'

'Who is this?'

'It's Claire Tanner, Mary. I'm downstairs.'

The phone went dead. A few minutes later, Mary was walking toward Reception, her manner exuding fury. She seized Claire's arm and led her out of the receptionist's hearing at a fast trot. 'What are you doing here?'

'Your brother asked me to come. He's worried about you.'

'Barry? You came all this way for Barry when you wouldn't come when I asked you?'

'Barry is paying me. You didn't seem able to do that.'

'You could have come and saved me the trouble.'

'And I would have, if you'd asked Barry to put up the money. Why didn't you?'

There was no answer.

'And I do believe you've landed your husband in a spot of bother. You do realise that you can go to jail for stealing that amount of money? Even when it's your husband you're stealing it from?'

'He won't press charges. He'd have to say who the money really belongs to and he won't want to do that. Look, I'm starving. I'm going to have breakfast. You can come with me, or you can wait out here.'

'I'll come with you. But I don't want anything to eat – I did rather well where I'm staying.'

Sitting at the table watching Mary eat breakfast, Claire studied her as closely as when they had first met. She would have been pretty once, in what Claire's mother would have described as a 'Woolworth Girl' way. She might even be pretty now, if she could shake off that look that said she was set against the world and the world was winning. She was a little overweight, but Claire didn't feel able to criticise anyone on that score. Her skin was a smoker's skin, wind-battered and reddened – but, once again, Claire would win no English rose contests. It was another warning to give up cigarettes herself. And she would – she was sure of that. But not right now.

Mary chose a breakfast from the menu as close to a British hotel's full English as she could get. She looked up at Claire. 'I don't think much of this bacon. Too skinny and too fatty. What did Barry ask you to do?'

Could something be skinny and fatty at the same time? Claire said, 'To find out what you were doing and keep you out of trouble.'

'Not to find Sally Varney and get her DNA?'

Claire shook her head. 'Have you found her yet?'

'No. But I will. That's what I wanted you to do – you're the private eye. Do you know where she is?'

'I don't. But I may, quite soon.'

'And you'll tell me?'

'I don't know, Mary.' Would she tell her? Barry Fitzgibbon was paying her – would helping Mary find Ellen Donovan be what Barry wanted her to do? She thought she would put that question to Barry before she made any decision about sharing information with Mary. And she remembered the last thing Fitzgibbon had said to her: 'Call me when you're in your Vancouver Island hotel room and we'll discuss the next move.'

At that moment, her phone made the intrusive jangling sound that said someone had sent her a message. As she looked at the screen, she was conscious of Mary, coiled like a cobra waiting to strike, staring at her. 'Well?' said Mary.

Was there any point in pretending the message hadn't been what Mary clearly hoped it had been? No, there probably wasn't. 'She's here.'

'On Vancouver Island?'

'In Victoria.'

Beside her, Mary had begun to relax. 'Close by?'

Claire put the phone in her handbag. 'I don't know. I'll look at a map when I get back to my hotel.'

'You need to make up your mind, Mrs Tanner.'

'Ms Tanner.'

'Well, whatever, but you need to make up your mind. Are you here to help me or to get in the way? Ellen Donovan isn't an unusual name. I found ten in Victoria alone, just by going through the phone book. My plan was to go and see them one by one until I recognised Sally Varney. But you can save me a lot of time. If you want to.' She took from her pocket a sheet of hotel writing paper with a handwritten list on it. Claire looked at the list. The one that had just been texted to her was on it, but she said nothing. Mary said, 'She's on there. Isn't she?'

Claire nodded. 'She's on there.'

'So. Are you going to tell me which one is her? Or do I have to go through the whole damn pantomime when you could save me the trouble?'

Claire thought about it. She said, 'I promised I'd call England when I got here. I think I need to do that before we go any further.'

'Because?'

'Have you given any thought to the danger you might be walking into? I mean, if you're right?'

'I can look after myself.'

'I wonder how many times those have been the last words anyone heard a person speak.'

'It isn't about that, though, is it? You didn't like me when I came to see you and asked for your help. And you don't like me now. Do you?'

It wasn't the sort of question you had to answer. Mary was right; she didn't like her now any more than when she had first met her, and she hadn't liked her then. But that wasn't the point. She said, 'That isn't the point.'

'You don't deny it, then.'

'I work for whoever pays me. That was never going to be you, and it isn't you now. I'll tell you which address is the Ellen Donovan you're looking for if Barry Fitzgibbon tells me to.'

A strange smile passed across Mary's face. 'And you're not going to tell me you like Barry any more than you like me.'

It was a statement and not a question, and Claire said, 'It isn't about liking. It's about the one who pays the piper getting to call the tune.'

'You could keep me out of danger by going to see her without me. Which is what I wanted you to do in the first place.'

'And if Barry…'

'…if Barry asks you to do that, that's what you'll do.'

Claire nodded in agreement.

'So how about you call Barry now? And then tell me what he wants you to do?'

CHAPTER 9

One of the most accomplished burglars within fifty miles of Chester, Terry Findlay had nothing but contempt for the kind of amateur who goes out in the evening looking for an empty house to break into. Terry burgled on commission. People with enough money told him what they wanted and Terry got it for them. He knew that he was at the top in his chosen career. Very little made him feel nervous and he had not been known to turn down any job, no matter how difficult the target. Yet now he stared at Bob Barnes with nothing in his expression that said he was going to refuse Bob's request – and yet, anyone who knew Terry could have told Bob just by looking at Terry's face that the answer was going to be no.

When Bob had stopped speaking, Terry left a long enough silence to be polite. Long enough to let it seem that he was giving Bob's proposition due consideration. Then he said, 'No.'

'Terry. You've no idea what I have riding on this.'

'That's your problem, not mine. What I have to think about is what *I* have riding on it. And the answer is, I could end up doing time. If I'm lucky. If I'm not, my wife and children never see me again. Sorry, Bob. I'm not taking that chance.'

'You don't think you could get in there?'

'I'm certain I could get in there. I can get in anywhere. What I'm not sure about is whether I could get out again without being caught. And I'm damn sure I know what those guys would do if they caught me turning their place over.'

'Please, Terry. I need that book.'

Still the unfathomable look on Findlay's face. He said, 'What I heard is that you need ten thousand quid. Is that what this is about?'

If Barnes had looked concerned before, some other word would be needed to describe his appearance now. 'Where did you hear that?'

'It's true, then. It's someone else who needs whatever story that book has to tell. And they'll pay you ten thousand? Plus the two thousand I'd want for going in there?'

Barnes shook his head. 'Your £2K comes out of my pocket.'

'You want my advice, Bob? Find some other way to raise the money. The only way you'll get someone to break into that place is by hiring a dickhead. And the dickhead will be caught. And before they dispose of him, they'll do whatever they have to, to get him to tell them who his customer is. And then they'll come and dispose of you. Won't your brother-in-law lend you the money?' When Barnes said nothing, the light of realisation came into Findlay's eyes. 'Of course. He's the one who wants the book. Forget it, Bob. Barry Fitzgibbon can call on enough muscle to survive a visit from those people. You can't.'

***

When Marie took the call from Claire, they exchanged some polite chat about Claire's journey and what she thought of Vancouver Island and then Marie transferred the call to Barry Fitzgibbon.

'Claire,' said Fitzgibbon. 'Good flight?'

'Can we skip the chat? I've done all that with Marie.'

'Suits me. What have you got to report?'

'I've met Mary. Her hotel isn't as nice as mine.'

'Mary doesn't have Marie's standards.'

'She's put together a list of all the Ellen Donovans on the island. It's a very big island, and a lot of Irish people have come to Canada over the years, so Donovan isn't an unusual name here and nor is Ellen. It's going to take her quite a while if she decides to knock on the door of every one of them – but the one she wants, the one who lives with Miriam Donovan, is on her list.'

'How do you know that?'

'Barry, I'm not going to share with you the details of how I gather information. Just accept that I know where the actual Ellen Donovan lives. All right? What I want from you is, do I tell Mary which Ellen Donovan is hers? Bearing in mind that she's going to go through each one of them and she'll find her eventually. Or do I go and check out the real Ellen Donovan on my own?'

Fitzgibbon sat in thought for a while. Then he said, 'How far is she from Mary's hotel?'

'Maybe half an hour in a taxi. And about the same from mine.'

'I see. And Mary isn't stupid, so I think we should assume that she'll check on the nearest ones before she goes further afield.'

'That's a fair assumption. In which case, it may help you to know that the Ellen Donovan she wants will be eighth on her list. So she may not get there today. But she may.'

'You've answered the question, then. Tell her where the woman is, let her go there alone, but watch her back. What's it like, this place where Donovan lives?'

'I looked at it on Google Earth. I'd say the Donovans are doing pretty well for themselves. It's quite a big house, it's surrounded by a fair amount of land, so it won't have been cheap, and it's on the waterfront, which I imagine jacks up the price quite a lot in a place like West Victoria.'

'Ellen has a lot to lose, then.'

Claire didn't respond. There was another of the silences that Fitzgibbon was not quite as good as Claire at, and then he said, 'Okay. Tell her what she wants to know, let her think she's going there on her own, but find some way to stay close. If you think she's in trouble, move in. In fact, if you think she's in trouble, it might be as well to call the police.'

'If ever there was a last resort, that's it. One last question. Your brother and Sally Varney had a child.'

'That's right. Tom.'

'How much of this does he know?'

'To the best of my knowledge, none of it. He's Jim's son but he thinks Jim and I are his brothers and Mary is his sister.'

'And you're sure of that?'

Although she couldn't see him, she sensed Fitzgibbon's shrug. 'He's in his thirties. I paid for him to go to the King's School and he went from there to Oxford. He was a rowing blue, thanks to the King's School rowing club on the Dee. He competed in the Boat Race.'

'What you're saying is, he's not stupid.'

'What I'm saying is, he's way above average. He may well have worked it all out by now. I don't know, because he's never said anything to me and I'm not going to raise the subject with him.'

'So it's possible he knows who his father is.'

'And that his father is in jail for murdering his mother. Yes. It's possible.'

* * *

When Claire had hung up, Fitzgibbon rang Bob Barnes. 'What prison is my brother in now?'

'Why do you want to know?'

'Don't be an arse, Bob. Just tell me. I know Mary visits him from time to time, so she must know, and I assume she tells you where she's going.'

'He's in Exeter.'

'Exeter! He couldn't be further away if he tried.'

'Two hundred and fifty miles. Mostly motorway, so you can do it in just over four hours as long as you drive at night.'

'How often does Mary get down there?'

'Not more than once a year, if that. Usually, she phones him.'

'Just like that?'

'Almost. You thinking of going?'

'I might be. I hadn't realised how far away he was. And I'd need a visiting order.'

'Phone him. You want me to give you the number? Mary keeps it right here by the phone.' He read it out loud without waiting for an answer and then said, 'This other business. I talked to Terry Findlay...'

'And he said no. I heard.'

'Dear God, does everyone know my business?'

'Probably, Bob. And if you talk on the phone like this, everyone will know mine, and I won't like that. If you're going to tell me you can't do the job I asked you to do, that's okay.'

'It is?'

'Of course it is. It was a long shot. You want something from me and I said I'd give it to you if you got the job done. The job doesn't get done, you don't get what you asked me for. That isn't too hard to understand, is it? But you don't talk out loud, on the phone or to anyone else, about what it is I want. I thought I'd make that clear.'

'Barry. About Friday...'

'I don't want to hear it. I offered you a deal. There is no other. One last thing. My brother...Tom. Does he ever visit Jim in prison?'

'Your brother Tom.' Barnes put just enough weight on the word 'brother' to convey that he knew the truth about that relationship. 'I never heard of him visiting.'

Fitzgibbon hung up the phone and then dialled the number in Exeter that Barnes had given him.

CHAPTER 10

The trackers Claire carried with her when she was working came in a variety of sizes and a range of appearances. One type was fitted into a ballpoint pen of sufficient quality that someone who found it in their possession would be unlikely to throw it away. When she sat down by Mary Barnes and told her to take out her list of addresses where people called Ellen Donovan lived, she handed her one of the tracker pens and told her which address to underline. Mary did that and offered to return the pen, but Claire said, 'Keep it. Someone gave me a bunch of them.'

'Thank you. They're nice pens. You're not going to add it to Barry's bill?'

'I'm not, no. Though I don't suppose you'd care if I did.'

Mary looked at the address she had marked. 'Are you coming with me?'

'Your brother doesn't want me to.'

'Wouldn't we be safer as a pair?'

'We might. We might not. But it doesn't matter, because your brother doesn't want me to go with you. And your brother...'

'...is the one paying your fee.'

'Exactly. So, while you're visiting Ellen Donovan, I'm going to spend the day looking round Victoria. Do your best not to get into trouble. You've got my mobile number. Is your phone charged?'

Mary took it from her handbag and looked at it. She shook her head.

'Might be an idea to fix that before you go anywhere. That would be just the thing, wouldn't it – to need to call for backup and to find your phone's dead.'

* * *

The tracker in the pen Claire had given Mary had enough battery life to last four days. When she had left Mary, she stopped at a coffee shop that advertised free Wi-Fi, connected her phone to Mary's tracker and watched Victoria go by as she drank her coffee. The sun was shining, people, for the most part, looked content with life and Claire was inclined to share that contentment.

Then, her coffee finished, she skimmed through her guidebook and accepted that the Butchart Gardens was not close enough to the centre of Victoria to allow her to respond in good time if Mary got herself into trouble. She decided to simply stroll around the town for a while to get the feel of the place. Her phone would let her know if Mary was on the move.

But nothing happened. Claire assumed that Mary's delay in leaving her hotel was to give her time to charge her phone. Good. In this civilised, attractive city it was difficult to imagine anyone being up to no good – but someone had been murdered thirty-two years ago and her body burned and, though that had not happened here, if Mary Barnes was right then the person responsible lived not very far from where Claire was standing at this moment. She decided to go back to her hotel; it would be easier to react from there if she needed to and it was, in any case, almost lunchtime.

But lunch was delayed because Claire found that jetlag was a bigger problem than she had anticipated. She set the alarm on her smartphone for thirty minutes from now, lay down on the bed fully dressed except for her shoes, closed her eyes and drifted off to sleep.

***

Having been turned down by Terry Findlay, Bob Barnes was now setting his sights a little lower. In fact, a lot lower. Glenn Farrell, known to his friends as Faz and to the police as an habitual drunk and occasional short-term guest in their cells, was not a burglar of the standard he had hoped to secure but looked like being all he could attract. Faz was staring at him through eyes that Bob might have wished reflected a little more intelligence. 'That's all you want? A book?'

'But the right book, Faz. The one with the customer names in it.'

'And if I bring you that, you'll pay me two hundred quid?'

'And all the beer you can drink all night long, Faz. But don't drink anything except tea before you go in there. There'll be alarms to deal with. You need to be sober.'

Glenn waved the warning away. 'Piece of cake, man. You're hiring a professional here. That's why you came to me, am I right?'

What Bob wanted to say was, *No, Faz, I came to you as the last resort. You are the most incompetent burglar for a hundred miles, which is why you've had three suspended sentences when my first choice, Terry Findlay, has never even been in court. It's also why I'm offering you peanuts instead of what I would have been prepared to pay Findlay. But I'm desperate. I need someone because if I don't have ten thousand quid on Friday I'm going to have to explain where their money has gone to people who aren't interested in explanations. And I may not see Saturday morning.* But there was no point in saying any of that, so he contented himself with a tired expression and a nod of the head.

'Anything else I pick up while I'm in there,' said Farrell, 'is mine? I can keep it?'

'Faz. I'm paying you two hundred pounds because I need that book. Any time you spend picking up other stuff is time you're at risk. If you see something you fancy, leave it where it is. Bring me the book. Get paid. Then go back and get it on your own time. Okay?'

Farrell nodded. Barnes had very little faith in the genuineness of that nod. But what was he supposed to do? When he showed Farrell out, he said, 'Tonight, Faz. And wait till it's dark. Okay? And everyone's left.'

Farrell looked a little puzzled. 'Left? Are you sure about that? Don't some of them live on the premises?'

'There's a flat upstairs and at the back, Faz. You have to wait till they go there. You'll know they've gone because all the lights will be out. Don't make a move till then. And be sober. You can get pissed off your face after you get back here with the book. All right?'

When Farrell had left, Barnes tried his wife's phone yet again. And yet again all he got was an invitation to leave a message. He said, 'Mary. You have no idea how much trouble you've landed me in. If I don't have ten thousand pounds to hand over on Friday, I don't have a Saturday to look forward to. Whatever you've got left, please take it to a bank and send it to me. I'll settle for six thousand – I can find the other four myself. You can keep the rest and we'll say no more about it. But please, Mary, if I mean anything to you at all, send me at least 6K.'

***

Her phone battery charged, Mary weighed her options. She could wait for Claire Tanner, the private investigator who'd refused to work for her but taken her brother's money and followed her here, to make contact. She could set off for the Donovans' house right now, on her own. She could wait until Claire made contact again and go in the knowledge that Claire was covering her back. Or she could go, but let Claire know that she was going.

That last option seemed the most attractive. If Barry was paying for her protection, let the woman he was paying earn her money. She keyed into her phone a message to say that she was leaving to visit Sally Varney, and that she was going right now, and she sent it to Claire. Then she set off.

The Donovans lived in West Victoria, which was some distance away, but she had Bob's money and she was in a hurry. She'd listened to his message, but there was no way she was going to find a bank and send him any money. He hadn't come through when she'd asked him, and she was going to give him exactly as much help as he'd given her. Apart from which, Bob always exaggerated. If he wasn't able to pay up on Friday, they'd give him some time. The alternative was that they'd end up with nothing. And what would be the point of that? Okay, they might rough him up a bit, but that was always a risk when you played with the kind of people Bob associated with.

She allowed her thinking to go a little further. Suppose he wasn't exaggerating? Suppose, when he failed to hand over the money they regarded as theirs, emotions ran away with them? Would it be the end of the world to be Bob Barnes's widow instead of his wife? If it came to it, she thought she could play that part. And so she took a taxi.

Here in Victoria itself, it seemed to Mary that a few opportunities were being wasted. There were an awful lot of condominiums close to the water, and a condominium couldn't have its own jetty. Presumably, that was why there were also an awful lot of marinas – but it seemed to Mary that, if you had the kind of money it probably cost to live on the shore, you would want to be able to walk to the end of your own garden and step onto your own boat. There didn't seem to be many places that offered that particular luxury.

And then she crossed over into West Victoria and things changed. There was no shortage of houses backing onto private jetties. It came as a bit of a shock when the taxi stopped and the driver said, 'Here you are.'

'This is the place?'

'This is the place. You haven't been here before?'

'No. I haven't. And I don't know how long I'm going to be here, so I wonder if you'd mind waiting?'

The driver looked thoughtful. Then he said, 'I will… But would you mind giving me fifty bucks right now? That will pay for the time so far and buy another twenty minutes. Then, if you don't need me after all…'

'Sure.' Now that she was here, she didn't want to be left completely on her own. She was just beginning to think about how wrong things could go. She handed over a red fifty-dollar bill with a picture of a boring-looking white man in a dark suit on one side and, on the other, a ship that looked as though it was surrounded by ice. 'A woman may turn up looking for me. Her name is Claire Tanner. If you see her, please tell her I'm in that house and I'd like her to wait here for me.'

'You got it.'

Then Mary walked up to the front door and rang the bell. Was this the stupidest thing she'd ever done? She thought it might be. But there was no way she was going home, tail between her legs, without going face-to-face with the woman she believed to be Sally Varney. She was here, and she was going through with it.

* * *

Claire's phone beeped to say Mary Barnes's text message had arrived, but Claire didn't hear it. The alarm she'd set went off, and repeated three times before giving up. Claire slept right through the noise. When she woke, five hours had passed. Hoping for the best but fearing the worst, she checked her phone. Mary had left the hotel a few minutes after Claire had fallen asleep. She'd gone to the house where Ellen and Miriam Donovan lived. She'd stayed there for about thirty minutes, and then she'd left.

Claire stared at the chart that showed where she'd gone after leaving the Donovan house. She wanted the information to be wrong. Because, if it wasn't, Mary Barnes was midway between Port Renfrew on the south-western coast of Vancouver Island and Neah Bay on the north coast of Washington State. If she was at sea, how did she get there? How was she travelling? And how was Claire supposed to follow her?

* * *

Four hours before Claire woke, two men had arrived at the back of the Donovan house in a twenty-one foot Bayliner. With a draught of less than three feet, mooring had been no problem. They'd got out of the boat and gone inside the house. Soon after that, a woman came out of the front door and spoke to the taxi driver. 'Thank you for waiting, but our friend doesn't need you to stay after all. How much do you need for your waiting time?'

'Twenty-five bucks, please,' said the driver, thinking he might as well make a little profit on the deal.

The woman handed over the money, the driver thanked her, and drove away.

CHAPTER 11

There didn't seem to be any option. It was not what Claire would have chosen, but it wasn't going to be a matter of choice. She would have to go to the Donovan house and ask what had happened to Mary Barnes. She consulted with the concierge, who told her a taxi was the only way and called one for her.

The woman who came to the door was not the one whose photograph Mary Barnes had shown her with the claim that her name was Sally Varney. Nor did she seem friendly. Claire said, 'I wonder if you can help me? I'm looking for Mary Barnes.'

'Yes? There's no-one of that name here.'

'Are you sure?'

The woman stared at her. 'You're asking whether I'm sure that some woman I've never heard of is not in my house?'

'She was very clear that she was coming here.' Claire thought she was pretty good at reading people's faces, but she was getting nothing from this one. At length the woman said, 'Perhaps you'd like to come in? And check?'

Was going into this house a sensible thing to do? What was the law on guns in Canada? They couldn't be as freely available as in America, surely? And if this really was where Sally Varney was living, and if that meant that

Sally Varney had conspired in the death and destruction by burning of another woman, could she be relied on to be someone who didn't break the law?

But there was no point in going through questions like that, because Claire knew going into the house was her job.

The woman waiting in the living room was the one on Mary Barnes's printout of a social media page. She looked questioningly at Claire. The other woman said, 'She's looking for...' She turned to Claire. 'What was the name again?'

'Mary Barnes,' said Claire.

The woman said, 'She didn't believe me when I said there was no-one here by that name. Did you ever hear of a Mary Barnes?'

The woman who might be Sally Varney shook her head. 'Never. When was she supposed to be here?'

'Within the last three hours,' said Claire.

The woman who might be Sally Varney repeated the shaking of her head. 'We haven't had any visitors for days. When was the last, Miriam?'

'Three days ago? Four?'

Claire said, 'There's someone else I'd quite like to find.'

'And who is that?' said the woman who must be Miriam Donovan.

'Sally Varney,' said Claire.

That got immediate recognition, but it wasn't what Claire might have hoped for. The woman who might be Sally Varney said, 'Not that again. Are you the nutcase who started this story running?'

'Nutcase?' said Claire. 'Story?'

Miriam Donovan said, 'We had the cops here. Not long ago – when was it, Ellen?'

'A couple of weeks,' said the woman who might be Sally Varney. 'They said a woman called Sally Varney had been killed in England years ago. And they said somebody over there had seen my picture on social media and claimed that I was the dead woman.'

Claire said, 'And are you?'

The ghost of a smile crossed the face of the woman who might be Sally Varney. 'Have you ever seen a dead person? They don't look like me. Trust me on that.'

Miriam Donovan said, 'Are you a British cop? Should you be here asking questions without someone from Victoria PD with you? Or maybe a Mountie?'

Claire shook her head. 'I'm not a cop.'

Miriam Donovan said, 'You're not, are you? What, then? A private eye?'

Claire said, 'Look. Since I'm here. Do you mind if I take a look round? Just to satisfy myself there's been no mistake? Someone is paying me to look after Mary Barnes and I like to give value for money.'

A look passed between the other two women and then Miriam Donovan said, 'Sure. Help yourself. You don't mind if we don't come with you? See, we know this woman hasn't been here and she isn't here now. But you go anywhere you like, open any closet you like, look under the beds, satisfy yourself.'

Fifteen minutes later, Claire had to admit defeat. There was no sign of Mary, and no indication that she had ever been here. She went back into the living room, where the two women appeared to be talking about something else and showed no sign of being in any way troubled. Miriam Donovan said, 'I hope you find her. I'm sorry we weren't able to help.'

'Thank you,' said Claire. 'I notice you have a little pier out there, but no boat. You don't have a boat?'

Miriam Donovan shook her head. 'It's the first thing most people think when they move into a place like this. You're on the water, you've got your own dock, which is what we call what you seem to call a pier, so what could be better than tying up your own boat there? But you soon find it's money wasted because you're almost never out on the water. And boats lose value each year, just like cars do.'

'You don't go fishing?'

'That's an interest that you either have or you don't. And we don't. Sure, we like to fill the freezer with fresh caught coho, but when the salmon are running there's a steady stream of First Nations people knocking on the door and offering all we can take at five bucks each.' While she'd been speaking, she'd been leading Claire toward the front door. She looked out. 'You didn't ask your cab to wait?'

Claire shook her head.

'I'll call one for you. Where do you want to go?'

'The Fairmont Empress.'

Miriam Donovan's eyebrows rose. 'The private-eye business must be paying well. Take a seat. I don't suppose you'll have long to wait.'

As Miriam Donovan was making the call, Claire tried one last trick. 'Sally Varney had a child by Jim Fitzgibbon. A boy. They called him Tom. He was raised by his grandparents. He thinks Jim is his older brother. He's thirty-three now. If Sally Varney is still alive, she must wonder what he made of his life. If I met her, I could tell her.'

And then the taxi was there. But not before Claire had seen the stricken look on Ellen Donovan's face. For the first time, she believed Mary Barnes might be right.

On the way back to her hotel, Claire tried Mary's phone again. She didn't expect the call to be answered, and it wasn't. She looked at the tracker and saw that the pen she had given Mary was still moving north in the sea off Vancouver Island. Whether Mary was with it was, of course, another matter.

Back at the Fairmont, she stayed long enough to get something to eat and then set off toward Mary's hotel. As before, the receptionist rang Mary's room. This time, the call was not answered. Wherever Mary was, she wasn't here.

* * *

After Claire's last sentence, the woman who said she was Ellen Donovan had walked out through the backyard and was standing on the dock, staring out to sea. Miriam Donovan wrapped her arms around her. 'That was a low blow, mentioning your son.'

'Do you think we did right? Letting her go?'

'We can't kill everyone who comes here asking questions, honey. Better to let it all die down.'

'Did it show? On my face?'

'That she'd got to you? It did. But what can she do about it? Tell the police she had an intuition? If they ask questions, you'll be ready for them.' She tightened her hug. 'But I know how you must be feeling. We could hire an investigator if you want. Find out what Tom is up to. But right now is probably not the best time.'

The woman calling herself Ellen Donovan nodded. 'Maybe.'

CHAPTER 12

Back in Chester, night had fallen and Glenn Farrell was attempting to earn two hundred pounds from Bob Barnes by burgling the building owned by Unity Corp, an organisation about which local people knew little. Which was exactly as the owners of Unity Corp wanted it. They'd arrived five years earlier from somewhere that varied with whoever was telling the story. For some, it was the Middle East and these people were hangers-on of ISIS who ought, by everything that was reasonable, to be in jail, or deported, or first in jail and then deported. For others, it was somewhere in Africa and Chester opinion could not decide whether it was a crime syndicate making money out of telephone and email scams or a centre of further education for students who had exhausted what was possible in their own countries. Then there were those who pointed at the southern states of the USA and said these were people who feared America was about to launch another war in which, this time, because of the nature of warfare today, it would be the educated who would be conscripted but the emphasis would still be more on the minority races than the whites – and they weren't having any of it.

Barry Fitzgibbon knew enough well-informed people of dubious moral standing to know that the accents were fake, that the people came from Harlow in Essex, that cocaine and heroin were delivered to them in bulk through a sailing centre on the Dee estuary, and that they sold it through a network that covered the whole country. Barry did not want to get into the business with them – since making his pile he had been assiduous in keeping himself and his activities clean – but he had a friend and one-time associate who had offered him a lot more than the ten thousand pounds he had promised Bob Barnes if he could lay hands on evidence of who the customers were.

It was, of course, a hopeless venture from the start, because who could ever imagine that drug dealers on this scale would record all their customers in a book? Even if they had, though, the book would not have come to light that evening through Faz's depredations because he was going about the burglary in the same cack-handed way he went about all his professional undertakings. He'd been in the building just long enough to locate, by flashlight, a filing cabinet that might, if he could only find a way to open it, contain what he was looking for, when the room was flooded with light and he was joined by three of the most unpleasant-looking men he'd ever set eyes on.

'You want to tell us what you think you're doing?' said one. The accent held no trace of the exotic origins Faz had heard people conjecturing about. Its sheer down-to-earthnesss gave him confidence that this was a minor problem out of which he could blag his way.

That was a mistake.

***

Claire was still pondering her next move when her phone rang and she saw her sister's name on the screen. 'Daisy! Daisy? Is something the matter?'

'Where are you?'

'I'm in Canada. Vancouver Island. It's work. A client sent me here to pursue a lead. Are you all right?'

'It's Jayden, Claire.'

Claire found breathing suddenly difficult. If that piece of shit had hurt her sister... 'What's happened?'

'He's been arrested. Claire, the police say they're going to oppose bail. I talked to Safia, Elliott Devons's girlfriend. He's the guy Jayden works for.'

That's right, thought Claire. *He is the loan shark Jayden beats people up for when they don't pay on time.* But she didn't say it out loud.

'Safia says Elliott Devons is looking for someone new. He doesn't think Jayden will get out. Not for years.'

All Claire could think about was the need to tread carefully. One wrong word and she could blow her relationship with Daisy for ever. She said, 'Have they charged him? Presumably not, if bail is still a possibility.'

'No. But Safia says Devons thinks they will. She says he thinks the police have everything they need.'

'What would the charge be, Daisy?'

There was a long pause before, very quietly, Daisy said, 'Murder. Safia says Devons doesn't think they'll even think about manslaughter. She says Jayden will get life. She says we should be thinking about a twenty-year tariff.'

In Claire's mind now was the thought, *If he gets life, you can get a life.* But, once again, she didn't speak the words. 'Do you know what happened?'

'No. Well, not exactly. It must have been self-defence – Jayden wouldn't hurt someone deliberately. And certainly not that badly.'

Sure he wouldn't. He hurt you deliberately. And more than once.

'I was hoping you could investigate. But if you're not here…'

'I'll ring Dewi Morgan. He'll find out what's going on.'

'Who?'

'A bailiff. Knows everything about everyone. He does a lot of work for me. Any time I want the inside info on something people would rather keep quiet, I call Dewi.'

'Thanks, Claire. I don't deserve you. You'll let me know as soon as you hear anything? The police won't even let me see him.'

He'll be on remand soon enough. You'll be able to see him then. But out loud she said, 'As soon as I know something, you'll know it. Take care of yourself, Daisy. I know you feel terrible, but you won't do Jayden any good by not eating properly or losing your job.'

'I know.' It hurt so much to hear the weakness in her sister's voice. 'I know. And our mother will never stop talking about it.'

'So don't tell her. We aren't little girls any more. There's no rule that says she has to know everything that happens. Stay away from Audenshaw, and don't answer the phone if she rings. Daisy, I have to go, I've got an emergency here, a lost woman who I'm very worried about. But before I do anything about that, I'm going to contact Dewi Morgan and get him on the job.'

'Okay, Claire. Good luck with your lost woman. I hope she turns up soon, and you can come back home.'

When she'd hung up, Claire sent a text message to Dewi Morgan, asking him to find out as much as he could as soon as he could. Then she called Barry Fitzgibbon's secretary. It was time she owned up to having lost the sister whose back he had paid her to watch.

CHAPTER 13

Detective Sergeant Harry Walford shrugged. 'I don't get it. Why are we interested? Some junkie OD'd on heroin, the ambulance service got to him in time, they treated him with naloxone, he's going to recover. Happens all the time. It's why ambulances carry naloxone with them. Why would we take an interest? We've got too many real cases as it is. Who is it, anyway?'

Walford's boss, Detective Inspector Julie Roberts, said, 'Glenn Farrell.'

'*Faz?* When did he start using heroin? I thought he was a beer man.'

'He is. He drinks in the Moor's Head. Bob Barnes has all sorts of bad habits, but he won't tolerate dealers in there. Where would a man like Faz get that amount of smack?'

'You think someone gave it to him? Tried to kill him?'

'Possibly the same someone that cut the tip off his little finger.'

Walford winced. 'Oh, shit. Oh, the poor bastard.'

'I don't think he was supposed to survive. I'm amazed he did, naloxone or no naloxone, when you consider the sheer volume of brown he'd apparently consumed. The paramedics must have got the naloxone into him pretty fast.'

'What does he say?'

'He's in a ward at the Countess of Chester. I've got a constable keeping watch, but the doctors won't let us speak to him yet. What Faz thinks of as his brain is floating somewhere with the fairies right now.'

'What do you want me to do?'

'He was dumped down by the Dee. Just past the rowing clubs and opposite Grosvenor Park. Get a couple of DCs down there doing door-to-door. Did anyone see anything? There aren't any houses, but there are buildings. Night watchmen. Security guards. Passers-by. Somebody did see something, because someone rang 999. Find the car that responded and see what they can tell you. Check with Control. And get someone looking at CCTV. I don't suppose whoever dumped him got there on foot. I'm going for coffee and a bacon sandwich while you get that started. Then you and I will go and see what his girlfriend can tell us.'

***

Marie took the message calmly enough, said she'd pass it on, 'and I'll call you back to tell you what Mr Fitzgibbon thinks the next step should be.' Claire was glad to get off the phone so quickly, because Dewi Morgan was calling her.

'It doesn't look good, Claire. And it's nothing to do with Elliott Devons. This wasn't work; Jayden Walsh picked a fight with a guy in a club in Manchester because he didn't like the way the guy looked at his woman.'

'Walsh's woman? But...'

'The woman wasn't Daisy, Claire. I don't know whether Daisy knows he's been two-timing her, but this was someone else. She lives in an apartment in Salford and it's Walsh who picks up the rent.'

'Oh. Oh, God. Oh, poor Daisy.' And yet, and yet... It would take Daisy a while to get over this, but what a joy if it helped her put the thug behind her. 'How long...?'

'He's been paying her rent for at least two years. I think she's also been working for him.'

'Working? Do you mean what I think you mean?'

'She's been turning tricks, and he's been finding the men she's been doing it with. Look, I don't want to ask this, but...'

'NO! I'm not going to believe that. My sister has acted like a mug where Walsh is concerned, but she hasn't done that. And I've no idea how she's going to react when she finds out about this other woman.'

'Well, it seems that when Walsh picked on the other guy he found he'd bitten off more than he could chew. It's the first thing life teaches you: don't pick a fight with anyone until you know who you're dealing with. It seems Walsh threw a punch at this guy, who turns out to have been Special Boat Services, and the guy didn't seem to notice he'd been hit. So then he returned the compliment and Walsh ended up on his knees. Blood all over the place according to witnesses, and all of it Walsh's. Then the guy takes the woman by the arm and marches her out of there. From what I can piece together, it seems he asked where she lived and she told him. If she was on the game, why wouldn't she?

'So when Walsh pulls himself together, he heads off to the woman's apartment. He doesn't know the special forces guy is with her, because no-one in the club has told him. They just wanted him out of there. He lets himself in and he hears noises coming from the bedroom so he checks it out. And there's the woman he thinks is his, on her back, and the guy's arse is going up and down on top of her. He goes into the kitchen, grabs a knife and cuts the guy's throat right where he is. Just picture it for a moment. All that blood – and where is it going?'

'All over the woman underneath him.'

'Exactly. Her face is covered in it, it's in her mouth, in her nose, she feels like she's drowning and she's screaming to wake the dead. Walsh tries to shut her up but it's too late – neighbours have called the cops. You know people say, "They've got him bang to rights," and you think, that isn't true, there's always a way out as long as you have a good enough lawyer. Well, there's no way out of this. They caught him red-handed – *literally* red-handed – and he's going down. And if you want my opinion, Daisy will be a lot better off without him.'

'Without question. But it's going to hit her hard before she realises that.'

'Well, she'll know by now, or if she doesn't she'll know very soon, because the police are going to be talking to her. Do you want me to contact her?'

Dewi had many qualities that Claire valued, but the tact to handle a vulnerable woman in a state of grief was not among them. 'No, thanks, Dewi. I have to do that myself.'

'Okay. You want a rundown on your other cases while I'm talking to you?'

'Is there anything urgent? Anything I need to know right now?'

'Nah. Everything is going the way you'd want it to go.'

'We'll leave it for at least another day, then. I have to try to get hold of Daisy as a matter of urgency.'

But when she rang her sister's number, it went straight to a recorded message.

***

The Bayliner was making good progress, heading north along the Vancouver Island shore. At the wheel was Miriam Donovan's brother, Max; his twenty-year-old son, Dane, was with him. Mary Barnes was still lying trussed up in the well in front of the cockpit, where they'd put her when they'd brought her out of Miriam's house, with tape sealing her mouth shut and plastic ties holding her ankles together and her wrists behind her back. Dane was looking more than a little unhappy. 'We're not going to kill her. Are we?'

Max shook his head. 'We are going to make it possible for her to die. I owe my sister that. But I don't owe her a murder.'

'So what…?'

'We'll drop her in Cape Scott Provincial Park. Let her take her chances. If she survives, it was meant to be. But the odds will be stacked against her.'

Dane was silent for a while. Then he said, 'What does Aunt Miriam think we're going to do with her?' When his father didn't answer, he said, 'She thinks we're going to kill her. Doesn't she? Do you know how sad you look sometimes when you talk about your sister?'

'Your aunt is a troubled soul. She always has been.'

'What has this woman done to upset her?'

'Miriam is very protective toward Ellen.'

'So we are doing this for Aunt Ellen, not Aunt Miriam?'

'Look. Ellen has done something that could mean serious trouble and the trouble would hit Miriam as hard as it would Ellen. Don't ask me what the something is that she did, because I don't know. I was very suspicious of Ellen when she first came to live with your aunt, but I've never tried to find out anything about her past because I suspect I'd rather not know. She did something; Miriam knows what it is and between them they've buried it. I'd like to leave it that way.' He gestured with his head toward the woman in the well. 'I can't bring myself to end her life.'

'But you can bring yourself to leave her somewhere remote. Is that because you think she'll be found?'

'Yes, I think she will. But not by people. We aren't going to leave her anywhere near San Josef Bay. We'll take her right round the cape and drop her well toward the eastern end of the park. If any people turn up to see her there, it will be a miracle. And we should not get in the way of a miracle. But I don't expect that to happen.'

'So… If not people…?'

'Bears have been very active in the park recently. And so have wolves.'

Dane went silent. They had turned the cape and were well on their way east before he spoke again. 'You'd leave a woman who means nothing to you to the mercy of bears and wolves? Not for your sister's sake, but for the woman she lives with. Who you say you never trusted. And you'd make me, your son, complicit? Have I got that right?'

There was a long pause. Then Max said, 'It isn't as simple as that.'

'So fill me in.'

Another pause. Then, 'I ran with some pretty dubious people when I was young.'

'Dubious?'

'Two of them were in the last riot in Oakalla before they closed it.'

'Oakalla?'

'Before your time. They called it a correctional centre. I don't believe it ever corrected anyone. And certainly not them. They're still locked up somewhere.'

'It was a prison?'

'And I could have been in there with them. It was me who... Well, you don't need to know that. It was a long time ago, I met your mother, I had a chance to turn my life around and I took it. The other guys were never going to rat me out. But Miriam... She knew. She's held it over me all these years.'

'Aunt Miriam knows something that could get you sent to jail?'

'For the rest of my life, Dane.'

'And to stop her telling, you're prepared to send a woman you never met and know nothing about to a place she will almost certainly not survive.' He let the silence run, but when it became clear his father had no more to say, he said, 'We're coming up to Barkley Sound. Put me ashore at Bamfield.'

'What?'

'I'm sorry, Dad. If you can't see that this is wrong, I can't help you. But I'm not going to be part of it.'

'What do you think you can do in Bamfield?'

'Theresa Fellini?'

'She was at school with you. What about her?'

'She's a marine biologist. Bamfield is where she works. She'll find a way to get me back to civilisation.'

'You won't tell her the story?'

'Not if you give me a hundred bucks so I can get home.'

'Dane...'

'Don't waste your breath, Dad. I love you to bits, but I'm not going to be part of killing someone.'

***

CCTV was no help in finding out who had dumped Glenn Farrell by the River Dee. It was not a much-used road and there were no cameras. Nor did anything come from door-to-door because the only security guards on duty had seen nothing until the police and ambulance turned up. Control, though, did have the mobile phone number of the young man who had called in the message, and Harry Walford went to see him. 'How did you come to be there?'

Jimmy Holmes licked his lips. It was obvious to Walford that he would have preferred to be having this conversation without his parents present, but Walford had no grounds to ask them to leave. It was their house, the boy had done nothing wrong and the presence of a responsible adult was required. After a pause, Holmes said, 'I just was. I mean, I was out there.'

'At that time of night?'

'I like to do that sometimes. Just go out on my bike and ride around in the dark.'

'Was anyone with you?'

'NO! I'm sorry, I mean no.' He sneaked a look at his parents. 'I was on my own.'

Walford glanced for a moment at the boy's father. It was obvious he didn't believe what his son had just said. It was also obvious that Walford could expect no help from him. 'So tell me what you saw.'

'It was what I heard. Moaning. No, not moaning – more like... You know, in a horror film, where something terrible is happening and someone is asleep except they're not asleep, they're surrounded by mutants and aliens and they know they're going to die... Like that. So I climbed over the fence and had a look and I saw this man and I rang 999.'

'And that's all you can tell me?'

The boy nodded. 'Yes. I'm sorry, but yes. Is he...?'

'He's alive, Jimmy. And if you had not been there and called us so quickly, he would have died. So well done. When it's all over, and we know who did it and we've arrested them, you'll come in for a lot of praise from our senior officers. I expect your name will be in the paper.'

'NO! I mean no. I don't want anybody to know.'

'It's sometimes difficult to get newspapers to see things the way we want them to see them, Jimmy. But, anyway, you can take a little private satisfaction from knowing that you saved that man's life.'

When Walford had gone, Jimmy Holmes senior said, 'You were with Judith Pashley. Weren't you?' His son looked at the floor. 'Well, son, I don't blame you for keeping quiet about that. Get the police interviewing Maurice Pashley's girl, Maurice is going to be round here having words with you.'

'I don't know who the hell he thinks he is,' said Jimmy's mother.

'Possibly. But he does fancy himself, and he thinks Judith is going to command something better than our son. I hope you used a condom, Jimmy. You get that one in trouble and you'll find out what trouble is.'

CHAPTER 14

Julie Roberts and Harry Walford presented themselves at the door of the maisonette in which Glenn Farrell lived with Niamh Hurley. Walford said, 'She knows he's in hospital. She also knows she won't be allowed in to see him any more than we are. We sent a family liaison officer to be with her, but Niamh told her to get lost.'

'I'm surprised that doesn't happen more often. Nice ordinary middle-class people who've encountered catastrophe for the first time in their lives imagine that the liaison officer is there to help them get through the pain, but people like Hurley and Farrell know better. It would be like inviting a spy into the house. I sometimes wish we could enforce their presence, but we can't.'

Hurley came to the door with a cigarette in her hand. The expression on her face could have been worry, it could have been sympathy for her partner in his hour of need, or it could have been something else entirely. She said, 'Any news? Is he going to live?'

'Do you mind if we come in?' said DI Roberts.

Hurley stepped back with some reluctance. 'If you have to. You won't find anything here.'

They weren't offered anything to drink and nor were they invited to sit. They ignored that by pushing onto the floor the stuff they found on two armchairs and sitting in them. Julie said, 'What time did Faz go out last night?'

'I've no idea. I wasn't here.'

'Of course not. And I suppose you've no idea where he was going? Or what he intended to do there?'

'None at all. I assume he was going to the Moor's Head. That's usually where he ends up. Have you asked Bob Barnes?'

'We'll be doing that next. You didn't become curious when he didn't come home?'

'Nah. He often doesn't come home. I assumed he must be hammered and he's sleeping it off somewhere. He always shows up in the end. Looking sheepish.'

'Niamh, can you think of any reason someone would cut off the tip of Faz's little finger?'

Niamh turned pale. 'Bloody hell. I had no idea… You're sure of that? I mean, it wasn't a stupid accident? You've no idea what he's like when he's pissed.'

'Unfortunately, a lot of the people we work with have only too clear an idea. They see him in that condition more often than sober. But, no. We are pretty certain someone did it intentionally. Presumably to get information out of him. It isn't nice to think of people like that here in Chester, so if you could rack your brains just a little to see whether you come up with any clue about where he might have been going, it might help us track down some very nasty people.' She glanced at Niamh to see what effect she was having. 'Nasty people who might be looking at people close to Faz, to see what other mischief they can get up to.'

Niamh did not spend much time in thought. 'He was going to break into that place – what's it called? Unity Corp.'

'You're sure? Why would he do that?'

'He was doing it for Bob Barnes. There was something Bob wanted out of there, and he was going to pay Faz two hundred pounds for it.'

'I'll ask you again. Are you quite certain about that?' When Niamh nodded, she said, 'Right. The sergeant and I are going straight to the Moor's Head to talk to Bob Barnes. Please don't phone him to say we are coming. If we treat that as interfering with the police in the execution of their duties, you'll be in court.'

'I called him when I heard Faz was in hospital. There was no reply.' She went with them to the door. 'Listen. I know Faz isn't much, but he's what I've got. Is he going to be all right?'

'Yes, Niamh, we think he is. As well as having a bit cut off his finger, he had enough heroin in him to kill a horse.'

'Heroin? Faz? No… You've got it wrong. Faz doesn't do drugs.'

'The suspicion has to be that the heroin was administered against his will. It was enough to kill him and I don't doubt that was the intention. But the paramedics got to him in time and filled him with naloxone. It may take a few days, but he'll be coming home. You might want to talk to him about being more careful what jobs he takes on. And who for.'

'You can count on it. The stupid bugger. It's time he got a proper job. We can't go on living like this.'

* * *

When the two detectives banged on the door of the Moor's Head a little later, nobody answered. DI Roberts said, 'Call the station. Let's get some strong lads with a big red key. I want to get in there.'

CHAPTER 15

Dewi Morgan was surprised to receive a phone call from the manager of a care home. They didn't usually struggle to collect fees. Or, if they did, they'd never in the past called on him for help. 'Mr Morgan?'

'Speaking.'

'I need to get this clear. Is that the Mr Morgan who came here with a young lady a few days ago to talk to Mr Bertram Musk?'

'Yes. That's me.' His first thought was that Musk had died, there were no relatives and an attempt was going to be made to get Dewi to take on the responsibility for burying or cremating the dead man. But that wasn't so.

'Thank heavens. Mr Musk was so eager to make contact. He wants to talk to you. Can you come here? And bring the young lady with you?'

'The young lady is, I believe, in Canada. She'll be back sometime next week. Would you like to ask Bert whether he wants to wait, or whether I will do on my own?'

'I'll find out, Mr Morgan, and I'll call you back.'

When she called back it was to say that Mr Musk would like to see Mr Morgan as soon as possible. But, when he got there, Dewi was greeted by a sombre-faced manager. 'I'm sorry,' she said. 'Mr Musk has good days and bad days. And I'm afraid, though this started out as a good day, it has deteriorated. Not surprising, I suppose, given his recent news.'

'News?'

'Oh, I'm sorry, of course, you don't know. I'm afraid Mr Musk's race is almost run. He's done incredibly well to get this far. It seems he faked his age in 1939 – said he was eighteen when he was only sixteen – but that still makes him ninety-nine now. We'd have held a party for him next year, but… He's been showing increasing signs… He went into hospital and they confirmed what our doctor thought. Cancer of the liver. Incurable. There's nothing they can do so they sent him back here, but we aren't equipped for someone in that condition. We are looking for a hospice bed for him.'

'Is that why he asked to speak to me and Ms Tanner, do you think?'

'Get something off his chest before he dies, you mean? There's no way of knowing, is there? At any rate, there's no point in putting you together today. Perhaps in a day or two? I'm sorry you've had a wasted journey. Would you like a cup of tea before you go? And I'll get Rio Wood to talk to you – he's the carer who's spent most time with Mr Musk.'

Rio Wood turned out to be a young man in his early twenties with a thin beard and an earring. He said, 'Just the last day or two, Mr Musk has wanted to talk.'

'I know he wasn't like that before,' said Dewi. 'I brought a visitor and he wouldn't say a thing.'

'Maybe that was it,' said Rio. He sighed. 'And maybe it wasn't. You can't tell. But you're right, he hadn't been a talker, and suddenly he was. I assumed it was because he sensed the end was near. But maybe something had reminded him of things he'd forgotten.'

'Did you spend much time with him?'

'We can't during our normal shift. There just isn't time.'

The manager said, 'This is not a private home, Mr Morgan. We rely to a great extent on government money. And there's never enough to hire the number of people we'd like, to give the amount of attention that is needed.'

Rio said, 'So I stayed on after my shift was over. And I just let him talk.' He looked up and smiled. 'He took hold of my arm and didn't seem to want to let go.'

'What did he talk about?'

'It was a jumble. He was talking about the past. I think he'd seen some bad things... I think he'd *done* some bad things, because... He talked about God. Did I believe in Him? Did I think there was a Judgement Day? I was there for about two hours and some of that time he just drifted. Like he was seeing things. Faces... People. Nothing I could make sense of. Something about a head. Something about a book. Something about security. "Made sure he knew he'd better not come after me" – that was something he said. And eventually he fell asleep, and I went home. Next day I don't think he remembered anything about it.'

Dewi stood up. 'Thank you, Rio. Here's my card. If you remember anything else, or if Mr Musk says anything else, please call me.'

'It's important, then? Not just the rambling of someone who knows he is about to die?'

'It could be, Rio. It could be. But let's not take a chance, eh?'

* * *

Ted Hughes answered the ring at his front door and found Tina Howard waiting on the step with a man of about his own age and a middle-aged woman. Something about the woman's appearance suggested she might be the man's daughter. Tina said, 'Ted. These people are looking for information. Their questions might interest you. May we come in?'

Ted led them into the sitting room. It wasn't tidy and they'd be able to smell his roll-ups, but what the hell? It was his house. He sat down and gestured for them to do the same.

Tina said, 'A few days ago, I sent Claire Tanner to see you about an interesting matter.'

'You did, and thank you. I think I was able to help her a bit.'

'Well, she's gone to Canada and that was partly a result of talking to you, so I guess you're right. The thing is, Ted, that these people' – and she gestured toward the two she'd brought with her – 'have come from Canada while Claire has been going in the opposite direction. They came to see me at the paper in the hope that we might be able to help them. And we might. It's just possible you might, too.'

Ted looked at the visitors, eyebrows raised.

The man said, 'Hello, Ted. My name is John Hubbick. I've lived in Ontario all my life, and so has my wife, but my father came to Canada from Chester right after World War II.' He nodded in the woman's direction. 'Nancy is my daughter. Her sister is Ellen. Ellen is missing and that's why we are here.'

Ted said, 'You think she's in Chester?'

'We don't know where she is. We haven't seen her for a little over thirty years.'

Ted said, 'This has all the hallmarks of a fascinating story. We're going to need a cup of tea. I could bring it in here, but life will be easier if we move into the kitchen. And will you find it unbearable if I light up? I know it's a disgusting habit, but it helps me think. I'll open the windows if that helps.'

Hubbick smiled. 'A disgusting habit I once shared. I've been free of it since the first of our children was born, but I wouldn't presume to tell you what you can and can't do in your own house.'

When they were in the kitchen, the tea had been made and Ted had lit his first cigarette, he said, 'Tell me about Ellen.'

'She was twenty-one. She'd just graduated from Waterloo University in Ontario. She planned to become a teacher, but first she wanted to take a year off and see something of the world. One place she wanted to see was Chester, because my father used to talk about it and she had cousins here. But then she vanished.'

Tina Howard said, 'We are putting a notice in the paper asking anyone who has any information about Ellen to contact us. But it's a bit more complicated than that.'

Hubbick said, 'We know Ellen reached Chester, because she met at least two of her cousins. One of whom saw her around town a few times.'

Nancy said, 'Not just around town. In Manchester, too. She was doing the club scene. It seemed like she'd made friends over here.'

Hubbick said, 'In her letters, she mentioned a number of girls. She seemed particularly friendly with one called Sally.'

'And of course,' Nancy said, 'Mom and Dad assumed that a friend was all Sally was. Her being a girl, and all.'

Hubbick said, 'Nancy makes it sound as though her mother and I are out of touch with today's world. And perhaps she's right. There were things that weren't talked about in Ontario when we were growing up there.'

Hughes said, 'Nancy, you think there might have been something between Ellen and Sally?'

'I have no idea. But I know my sister.'

'Better than anyone,' said Hubbick. 'Including their mother and me. When she first left, Ellen wrote to us every week. They had cell phones in 1990, of course, but they were nothing like they are now and most people didn't carry one. Once in a while she'd say where she was going to be and we'd phone her there. We were happy to pay the cost of the call. She was our daughter, after all, and off on a big adventure.'

He came to a halt and wiped away a tear. Seeing her father's difficulties, Nancy said, 'At first, the letters were full of news. She told us everything she was doing and who she was doing it with. But that changed. I was away at college myself, but I talked to Mom and Dad every week and I could tell how worried they were becoming. So I wrote to Ellen at the last address we had for her. Which was here, in Chester. I wasn't coming the heavy sister act – just, you know…I'm here, you're there, this is what's happening for me, what's happening for you?'

'She didn't answer?'

'She did. She told me life had changed for her and she was cutting herself off from the family for a while. Maybe she'd be in touch again, maybe she wouldn't – but she'd met someone, nobody Mom or Dad would be able to approve of, and she didn't care. She was moving away from Chester because she wanted a new start. She said this guy she was with was an engineer. He worked abroad most of the time and she was going with him. I wrote back saying "Don't cut me off, you'll always be my sister, I'll always love you," all the rest of the stuff you'd expect me to say. She didn't reply.'

Her father said, 'We never heard from her again.'

Ted said, 'That letter she sent you, Nancy. Did you…?'

Nancy took from her bag a folded piece of paper so well-thumbed that it looked as though it was wearing through in places. She handed it to Ted.

Ted said, 'It's typed.'

'Exactly,' said John Hubbick. 'And she's only signed with the single letter "E". It was so unlike her, we thought what you're probably thinking: *there's no way Ellen wrote this. Something's happened to her.* So we hired a private investigator. It cost us a lot of money. More than we could afford, really. But we were desperate for news. If she didn't want to talk to us for a while we could live with that, but we needed to know she was all right. But the investigator came over here and talked to the cousins who'd seen her and somehow he found a relative of the man they'd seen her with, and he sent us this report.'

Ted opened the folder Hubbick had handed him. The first thing he saw was the invoice – an eye-watering figure even thirty years later. 'This is the investigator's name? Eugene Cohen?' Hubbick nodded and Ted said, 'He says he tracked Ellen down. He says she told him the same thing that was in that letter you had, Nancy. That she was with an engineer, that he was going abroad to work, but she was going with him...'

'...and that she wanted to have nothing further to do with anyone in Ontario,' said Hubbick. All these years later, the despair was still visible in his eyes. 'We couldn't believe it. But we had to.'

'He doesn't give the engineer's name.'

'He said Ellen had refused to give it to him. She said the engineer had gone to Saudi Arabia and she would be following him. She said her life was her own business and no-one else's and we should mind ours.'

'You accepted that?'

'No, of course we didn't accept it – you don't let your own child cut herself off from you, however much she may want to. We asked Cohen to do his best to check. He was able to make contact with a private investigator in Riyadh. You'll find that report in the file. It's in a fairly odd form of English, but you can understand what it says.'

Ted browsed until he found the document. While he was reading it, Hubbick said, 'He says there are lots of engineers in Saudi Arabia from Britain and elsewhere in the West. He says they live in gated communities. He says he couldn't find anyone who recognised the photograph we'd given him, of what Ellen had looked like just before she left Canada, and nor did the name Ellen Hubbick ring any bells. He says how much it would cost to investigate every single Saudi location that had Western engineers working there. It was a huge sum and we'd already spent more than we could afford. It will seem like we gave up, but…'

Ted nodded. 'I understand. An investigation like that could go on for a long time, bankrupt you, and still not find the person you were looking for. So you left it?'

'We felt we had no choice. We hoped Ellen would come to her senses and make contact. But thirty years have gone by and we haven't heard a word.'

Nancy said, 'You'll be wondering why we are here now. My mother has Alzheimer's. She is in a home. We don't know how long she has left, but she still has occasional moments when she seems to be in the same world as the rest of us, and when that happens she calls for Ellen.' Her voice broke on the last words. 'We're desperate to find my sister, tell her about her mother, and get her to come home even if it's just long enough to say goodbye.'

'I understand. Are you married yourself, Nancy?'

'Wayne and I celebrate twenty-five years later this year. That's another reason to get Ellen home. She should have been my maid of honour. She missed that, but she could be there for the silver wedding. She could bring the engineer with her, if he ever existed.'

'You doubt that?'

'As I said earlier, I know my sister. If she's with someone, it's more likely to be a woman than a man.'

'And she could bring the woman,' said Hubbick. 'Ontario has done some catching up over the years.'

'Okay. I'd like a word with Tina on her own, if that's okay.' When Nancy and her father began to stand up, he said, 'That's okay – you stay there. Tina and I will go into the back garden.'

They sat on an ancient swing seat. Ted said, 'You haven't told them what took Claire to Canada.'

'I had reservations... Tell them that and what are they going to do?'

'You don't think they have a right to know?'

'It isn't straightforward. Is it? They could shoot off to Vancouver Island, beard this Ellen Donovan in her den, and find out she is nothing like Ellen Hubbick.'

'Apart from which, what journalist is going to get first dibs on the story if it is her?'

'You fill me with shame.'

'It doesn't show on your face. But if you haven't told them, I'm not going to. I'll give this some thought, Tina. And Claire left her card with me. I might very well see if I can get her on WhatsApp.'

'WhatsApp!'

'Don't ever let anyone tell you you can't teach an old dog new tricks.'

***

There was no-one in the public bar of the Moor's Head when the battering ram had secured their entry. The private back room was a different matter. The chair Bob Barnes was tied to had fallen backward onto the floor but it looked as though Bob had probably been dead before that happened. His naked body was marked by a number of cigarette burns, some of which were on his testicles. As Harry Walford squeezed his legs together and winced, DI Julie Roberts pointed to pieces of finger and toe scattered on the floor. 'They've really done a number on him. Call it in. Get SOCO here and tell one of those uniforms to hang some crime scene tape. I expect they'll want to second us, but this is one for the Major Investigation Team.'

At that point they heard a woman's raised voice asking what had happened to the door, followed by a violent, high-pitched screaming. Julie Roberts turned. 'What the hell? Who are you?'

A uniformed officer had followed her in and was attempting to lead her away. 'Sorry, ma'am, she slipped past us. I think she's the cleaner.' He looked at the scene in the back room for the first time. 'Bloody hell!'

'Well, get her out of here. But don't let her go home. We'll want to talk to her. Come on, Harry – we shouldn't be in here without coveralls, boots and hats. Whoever comes in as crime scene manager is going to have a fit if they find us trampling over the evidence.'

***

It was well after midnight and dark as only a place where no human walks can be dark. And then cloud moved away from the full moon and the scene was bathed in silvery light. The boat had slowed, and they hadn't seen anyone else, either at sea or on the shore, for some little time. Max cut the engine. Then he set about snipping the cable ties from Mary. He said, 'You don't smell too good. Have you pissed yourself?' He moved a little closer. 'I don't think that's all you've done.'

There wasn't any doubt that that was fear in Mary's eyes. Fear and… Just a little hope? Hope that, if he was going to kill her, he'd have done it by now? She said, 'Where are we? And what are you going to do?'

'I'm going to put you ashore.'

'Ashore?' She looked at the nearest land. It would not have been a welcome sight for a fit woman with a passion for walking in the wilderness. For an overweight city woman who smoked and thought opening a newspaper was exercise, intimidating did not begin to describe it. She said, 'Here?'

'Here. That land you're looking at is part of the Cape Scott Provincial Park. And along that shore runs the North Coast Trail. If you're going to meet anyone, it will be on the trail. It's forty-three kilometres long and if you go that way,' he said, pointing to his right, 'you will end up in San Josef Bay. There are buildings there with people in them. You will even get something to eat. But if I were you, I'd wait until morning because walking through trees like that in the dark is not a good idea.'

'And if I don't get there?'

'Why would you not? Forty-three kilometres is twenty-five miles as near as makes no difference. Surely you can walk twenty-five miles if you need to. Make an early start, you'll be there in time for lunch.' He thought it best not to mention that the guidebook suggested allowing five days for those twenty-five miles. The terrain was so challenging, friendly governments used it to train special forces. 'They do decent burgers at San Josef Bay. You're not a veggie, are you? And they'll have good salmon.' He took the mobile phone from her bag and threw it into the sea. 'You won't need that. That would be cheating.'

'Why are you doing this?'

'Miriam Donovan is my sister. She thinks you need to be taught a lesson. What we both hope is that when you emerge from those woods you will have a more sensible approach to her and her friend. Now it's time for you to go ashore.'

She shook her head. 'No. I don't believe a word you've said. You're not leaving me here.'

But she was neither big enough nor strong enough to resist, and the next thing she knew she was in the air and over the side of the boat. Then she was in seawater up to her waist. Max said, 'I saw you had cigarettes in that purse. Hold it up high so they don't get wet. You'll want to smoke while you wait for it to get light again.' And then he touched the throttle and turned the wheel to head out to sea once more, leaving the hapless Englishwoman to wade to land.

Smelling like that, she'd attract bears and wolves. And coyotes. Coyotes also lived there. Of course, people walked those trails. Fit, healthy people. People who loved being in the wilderness and knew what you had to do to survive there. How to camp safely in bear and wolf country. Not people like the one he'd just dumped there. She really had no chance at all. But it was what it was. Sometimes you have to choose: family or a stranger?

***

Claire had thought back to her time as a journalist and decided that the help of the press was what she needed here. And one thing you can say about journalists: it's never hard to find one. Just make for the nearest newspaper office.

The reporter assigned to her was friendly but made clear the limits to what she was offering. 'I can push the missing person aspect. A woman visiting Canada from Europe has disappeared, and it's up to friendly, helpful Canadians to do everything they can to find her. I'll even mention that she was carrying a tracker – I won't say she didn't know she was; I'm not sure about the legality in Canada of what you did there – and that the tracker appears to have moved up to the very eastern part of a remote provincial park. What I won't do is make any suggestion of abduction. Nor will I mention that she was in pursuit of a woman living here who may or may not have been murdered more than thirty years ago. If I did, the editor would spike it. I took the liberty of googling your past, Claire. I think you'll understand why we wouldn't want to risk a lawsuit.'

Claire nodded. Was she ever going to get away from the mistake that had ended her career in journalism?

The reporter was standing up. 'We'll get it out there as soon as possible, which means this evening's edition. If we hear anything, I'll call you.'

'You could include, in the story, the hotel where I'm staying. Then people could contact me direct.'

'Yes, Claire, we could do that. But then we'd risk being cut out of any interesting developments in the story. So I think we won't.'

It seemed that was the best she was going to get. And, as she left the newspaper office and turned her phone back from silent to normal, she saw that she'd had two calls. One was from Barry Fitzgibbon's secretary and the other was from Daisy. Marie's message was straightforward: 'Please wait in your hotel. You will be visited there by a Canadian investigator, Eugene Cohen. He has Mr Fitzgibbon's complete confidence.' Daisy's had been delivered in tears and simply said, 'Please call me.'

Walking back to the Fairmont Empress, she called her sister. The tears were still there. 'Claire. He's had another woman. All this time, he's had another woman. And it was her he killed someone over.'

'I'm sorry, Daisy. I...'

But something in her tone of voice had alerted Daisy. 'You knew. Didn't you? You knew.'

'Dewi Morgan told me. I tried to call you straight away, but there was no answer.'

'Oh. I suppose you're glad.'

'Glad? A man has been two-timing my sister and he's broken her heart and I'm supposed to be glad? How the hell would that work?'

The sobbing had died away to a quiet whimper. Let her get it all out – she'd be better for it in the end. 'You never liked him. Did you?'

'Oh, Daisy, I didn't dislike him or like him. I hated the way he treated you. How he hit you. It's never all right, Daisy, for a man to hit a woman.' *And I didn't like the way you let him, or made excuses for him, and didn't just walk out on him.* But this was not the time to say that.

'He'll go to prison, Claire. Probably for a long time.'

Yes, he will. And one day you'll see that that's what he deserved.

'I won't visit him.'

Thank God for that. 'You won't?'

'I never even thought about being disloyal to him. And he's been cheating on me since the beginning. I need to start putting him out of my mind. Getting him out of my system.'

Oh, you do, you so do.

'When will you be home? Did you find the missing woman?'

'Not yet. I'm hopeful I might know roughly where she is. And I'll be home just as soon as

I can. We'll have a girls' night out. You and me against the world. We'll flaunt it.'

'I'd like to do some flaunting. But not yet. I know I've behaved like an idiot. I don't need to look at other people and know that they know it, too. Let's start with a girls' night in. You, me and a bottle of wine. With another one as backup. We'll get a take-away so neither of us has to cook. And you can tell me how stupid I've been over Jayden.'

'I'll never tell you that, Daise.'

'Daise! You haven't called me that in so long.'

'We won't be talking about anything to do with the past. We'll be focused on the future.'

She became aware that Daisy was laughing. It would have seemed impossible even a few minutes ago, but it was there, if slightly hysterical. Then Daisy said, 'Do you remember when you rang? And I pretended that you were someone claiming to be from Microsoft, so that *he* wouldn't know who I was speaking to? And I knew you had the brains to get the message. Brains. That something Jayden never had. And thanks to him, I forgot about mine. Well, that's over.'

Thank God. But she isn't going to say that.

Chapter 16

The Major Investigation Team had slid into action. Detective Chief Inspector Sylvie McIntyre was senior investigating officer and the machine had gathered round her some of the best detectives in the force's area. All of them had tasks recorded on HOLMES, the Home Office Large Major Enquiry System, and were out on the street, ticking them off.

To DI Julie Roberts and DS Harry Walford, McIntyre had assigned a task she saw as central to the investigation. 'We all know the three questions we need answers to. Why this person? Why here? Why now? Answer that and you're well on the way to knowing who did it. The Moor's Head has been known to this force for years – was known to us long before Bob Barnes bought it. We know the kind of people who use it. Some of them will have a damn good idea what Barnes did to upset somebody so badly they cut off his digits and stubbed cigarettes on his balls before they killed him. You two talk to as many of the pub's regulars as you can and find out what people are saying. Start by finding out the latest from SOCO. I should think the forensics in that place are going to be very interesting. And Barnes was married, right?'

'To a Fitzgibbon,' said Julie.

'She doesn't seem to have been there when her husband was killed. Find her, get her alibi and check it. A Fitzgibbon girl, she must know some of the least savoury people in town. If she wanted her husband killed, she'd know who to ask.'

***

Back in her room at the Empress, Claire felt at a loss. The story of the missing Mary Barnes would hit the streets shortly and until she heard from Eugene Cohen there seemed little she could do. Then her phone showed a message from Ted Hughes. Check your email She was just about to fire up her laptop and do that when reception called to say a Mr Cohen was downstairs. In her present mood, talking to someone seemed more active, more productive, than reading emails. Making a mental note to log on as soon as possible, she went downstairs.

***

'Find her,' the DCI had said, but finding Mary Barnes proved not to be straightforward. Terry Singh was crime scene manager, responsible for the scenes of crime team that was still turning the Moor's Head over. A place where someone has been murdered automatically becomes a crime scene. The advantage of that to the police, in this case, was not just that they could put their forensics experts in without needing a warrant or clearance from a senior officer. It also meant they could look for and take possession of evidence of any wrongdoing and not just matters concerned with Bob Barnes's murder.

Terry said, 'We've unearthed all sorts of stuff that we'll be passing to the DCI. CID arc going to be able to clear up a number of crimes they didn't even know had been committed. But for you, there are two things in particular you need to look at.' He showed them a transparent evidence bag containing a picture of a woman. 'We've given the forensic IT team the laptop that we think printed this and I've no doubt you'll be able to get more information from them. But there's a handwritten addition. See?'

Julie Roberts said, 'It looks like "Sally Varney". Right?'

'That's what we thought. It wasn't a name that meant anything to me or anyone else on the team.'

'Or to me,' said Julie.

'So we checked it. Mary Barnes has two brothers. One is Barry Fitzgibbon, who I don't think anyone would trust but who appears to lead a blameless life. The other is Jim Fitzgibbon.'

'Isn't he the one serving life for murder?'

'He is. And the person he murdered was Sally Varney.'

Harry Walford had been keying information into his tablet while this conversation went on. He said, 'Boss, you need to hear this. I entered Sally Varney into NICHE. Mary Barnes came into the station three weeks ago and said she'd found a photograph on social media of the woman her brother was jailed for murdering.'

'Did she, by God? And what did we do?'

Walford scrolled down the NICHE entry. 'The officer she saw said she'd need more evidence before she passed it to CID. Her notes say Mary Barnes didn't present any pictures of Sally Varney herself, so there was nothing except Mary Barnes's word to say that this was her.'

'Can't argue with that.'

'The notes also say that if Jim Fitzgibbon was found guilty of murder someone must have been dead. There must have been a body.'

'Or that.'

'We didn't give up completely. The officer sent the picture to Canada for investigation by the police there. They came back four days later to say the woman in the picture was called Ellen Donovan, she'd never been in England, and she'd never heard the name Sally Varney. At which point the job was closed on NICHE.'

'Okay. We need to find Mary Barnes and see what she has to say. Terry, you said there was a second thing?'

Singh produced another transparent evidence bag, this one containing a notebook and two books of bank paying-in slips. He also handed Julie a sheet of paper. 'I'd rather you didn't handle these until they've been processed. But I've copied some entries for you.'

'Tell me what I'm looking at.

'There are two paying-in books. It will need to be confirmed with the bank, but it looks to me as though one of them is for cash receipts in the usual run of business, while the other one...' He pointed at the notebook. 'That notebook holds a record of amounts of cash and dates. It doesn't say where the money came from – presumably Bob Barnes knew and didn't need to remind himself.'

'That suggests it all came from one person.'

'One person, one company, one source – whatever it was, there was likely only one. I've listed the amounts and the dates on this piece of paper. Beside them, I've given the dates they were paid into the bank using the second paying-in book. The record is very regular.

The money was received every Monday and by the end of that day it was in the bank, less ten percent. I have no evidence for this, but I'm guessing that Barnes was handling the cash for someone else and taking ten percent as his commission.'

'It wasn't the money from the bar takings? With the deduction being to reduce his taxable income?'

'It doesn't seem so, because the other paying-in book also shows regular deposits on Monday and they are higher than on other days. I imagine takings were always better at weekends than during the week.'

'Okay. So...'

'According to the notebook, he should have been depositing about ten thousand pounds on Monday. And he didn't. Not on Monday and not on a subsequent day. That was the first time he ever failed to make a deposit on the Monday he received the cash.'

'So it seems fair to assume...'

'You're the detective. I leave deduction to you. But look at it. Every Monday, someone hands Bob Barnes a big chunk of money. The same day, without fail, Bob Barnes deposits it in the bank.'

'Looks like money laundering.'

'Exactly. Pubs are cash businesses, and cash businesses provide excellent cover for people who have money they shouldn't have and want to get it into the system so they can legally use it. But then, one day, he doesn't make the deposit. And three days later, on Thursday, he is killed.'

'Killed in such a savage and drawn-out way, someone might have been trying to get him to say what he'd done with their money.'

'It seems at least possible,' said Singh. 'You won't know for sure till you find out who was giving him the money.'

'Which we need to do as soon as possible. I don't suppose you have any help to offer there?'

'Sorry. We've collected a lot of fingerprints and some DNA. We haven't been able to identify any of the DNA yet, and the problem with fingerprints is what it always is: they tell us someone was here but they don't say when. But when we get the reports back, we'll make sure the DCI has them immediately.'

CHAPTER 17

Mary stood on the shore. The tree line behind her was forbidding: impenetrable, dark – and who knew what eyes might be watching her from there? She'd shouted as the Bayliner moved away, screamed in fact, begging Max to come back, promising silence, promising anything he asked – just please, please, don't leave her here.

But he'd sailed on. She'd watched, praying for the first time she could remember. Praying that he'd come back. Praying that she'd be spared. Praying for anything that would get her off this stretch of white sand.

It was a clear night, which was just about the only thing going for it. Apart from the moonlight, in this place, where no lights shone on earth to filter the view, the dark vault above her was studded with stars. It could have been a night of wonder. All it needed was a hotel, and a pool, and waiters bringing drinks, and the company of someone to love.

It was a time for asking herself questions. But the questions in her mind were questions she had no answer to. Why, if she was going to think about being with someone she loved, had she ever married Bob Barnes? How could she have set her sights that low? And why had she put up with him all this time? If she ever got out of this, the first thing she was going to do was to demand a divorce. Get him out of her life. If she ever got out of this... But what chance was there of that?

And then there was the bigger question. Why had she come here? If that was Sally Varney in the house on the Victoria waterfront – and she was pretty sure it was – then her brother Jim had served thirty-two years in jail for a crime that hadn't been committed. But there'd been a body, she knew that – so someone had died. If not Sally Varney, then who? And even if Jim had not been the killer, if he'd been set up, if he'd taken the fall for someone else as he had always claimed, did it matter all these years later? Barry said Jim was in no state now to be on the outside. That the time to rescue him was gone. It was true, life was a bastard – but she'd always known that. You can't be a Fitzgibbon, and you especially can't be a female Fitzgibbon given the second class, subordinate role Fitzgibbons assigned to women, and not know it.

She shivered. She wasn't dressed for this and it was even worse when her clothes were wet. Wet... And, she had to admit, soiled. And she hadn't eaten since breakfast and she was hungry and she was thirsty. There was nothing she could do about the hunger and the thirst, though in a little while she would smoke a cigarette, which might keep the hunger at bay, but she could do something about the filthy state of her clothes. Placing her bag where the sand was dry, she stripped below the waist, waded into the sea, rubbed her knickers in the salt water and then, a little more gently, washed her own nether regions. Then she came back to the shore, laid out her washing in the hope that it might dry, and sat down with her back against a boulder.

She lit a cigarette. As she drew the smoke deep into her lungs, she remembered the cigarette she had smoked in the backyard at Claire Tanner's private investigator's office. She wished with all her heart that she'd never been near Claire Tanner. That she'd never connected Ellen Donovan's photograph with Sally Varney. That she had minded her own business and left sleeping dogs where they lay.

And then she heard a low growl. And movement. And she knew with certainty that more than one pair of eyes were fixed on her.

***

Claire's conversation with Eugene 'Call me Gene' Cohen began in a way that Claire was familiar with from meeting other private eyes. Who were they dealing with? Could they trust each other? Even if they could, could either of them rely on the other person's skill? Eugene seemed taken aback when Claire said she had no licence.

'I don't need one. Licences are issued by the Security Industry Authority, and I don't do security work. I would only need a licence if I intended to work in close protection, or as a bouncer at a premises that sold alcohol. I don't. How did you come to know Barry Fitzgibbon?'

'I think what you want to know is how did Barry Fitzgibbon come to know me. I did a job for him. How he found me, I don't know – Yellow Pages, maybe. And I'm sorry, Claire, I can't tell you more than that. You know what this business is like. Let it get around that you breached someone's right to confidentiality, you're finished. People stop calling. And I can't afford to have that happen. But people do come to me – I've been around a long time. Your father is probably about my age...'

'My father is dead.'

'There you are, then. I started out as a cop back home in Ontario. Didn't get on with the people I needed to get on with. I'm sure it's different in the big cities, but in little country towns like the one I grew up in there's an understanding that the people with the money get away with things that other people go to jail for. Become a cop, you're expected to smooth the way for people who have the power to return the favour. I couldn't live with that. So I left and became a private investigator. That meant I had to leave Ontario, because in this country you do need a licence, and it's issued by the province you want to work in. There were people who had both the will and the power to block mine in Ontario. I don't speak French, which ruled out Québec, and east of there is a bit parochial. They like strangers when they come as tourists spending money, but they can be a bit difficult about doing business with you. That meant choosing between the Prairie Provinces and BC. Spend a winter on the prairie and you'll see why I chose British Columbia.

'Tell me about Barry's sister.'

CHAPTER 18

Julie Roberts told Harry Walford to send the HOLMES receiver a note saying they couldn't find Mary Barnes and asking if a new task had been assigned to them. A reply came back almost instantaneously asking Julie to call the DCI.

Sylvie McIntyre said, 'Glenn Farrell has regained consciousness and we can speak to him. You were first on the scene, so please go to the Countess of Chester and see what he has to say.'

'Okay, boss. His wife says he was going to break into Unity Corp. You want us to interview him under caution?'

'Why not? A caution might make him think. And she says he was working for Bob Barnes, so tell him about Barnes being killed. That might help him understand he's in over his head and he needs our help. Wear body cameras so you can film him and record the conversation. What we want is something that provides a reason to call Unity Corp a crime scene and get SOCO in there. Do your best – and let me know how it goes.'

When Julie had cautioned him, Farrell said, 'What the hell are you talking about? Someone has tried to kill me and you treat me as if I was the criminal here.'

'We understand that you were hired by Bob Barnes at the Moor's Head to burgle Unity Corp.'

Farrell's immediate look of shock was rapidly replaced with one of ridicule. 'Where on earth did you get that bullshit?'

'From your partner, Faz. From Niamh Hurley.'

Now the shock was back. Farrell opened his mouth to say something, then closed it again.

'And something else you should know, Faz, is that Bob Barnes is dead.'

'Bob? Dead? How?'

'Well, that's the interesting thing. Somebody cut off the tip of your finger. Somebody cut off all of Bob Barnes's fingers. And his toes. Does that suggest anything to you, Faz?'

Farrell's face had faded to the deadest white. 'Am I protected here? Have you got someone guarding me?'

'I see you've come to the same conclusion as we did. That the person who put you in here and the person who killed Bob Barnes are one and the same. And that, since they didn't expect you to survive, when they hear you *have* done they may very well come back to finish the job.'

'I asked if you had someone guarding me.'

'We are short of people, Faz. You know how it is – years of underinvestment in the police, whatever government happens to be in power. If you want us to provide protection for you, what have you got for us in return? Starting with, why did you break into the premises occupied by Unity Corp?'

All signs of scorn and resistance on Farrell's part had disappeared. 'Bob Barnes asked me to. He said there'd be two hundred quid in it for me if I brought him a book he wanted.'

'A book? Couldn't he just go to the library?'

'Not that sort of book. He wanted a list of people who dealt with... Whoever it is that's in there. You hear all kinds of stuff about that place, most of it obviously rubbish. But this book was worth a lot of money to Bob Barnes.'

'I wonder why?'

'Don't you people have officers under cover?'

'Well, if we do, we're not going to tell you about it, are we? That would defeat the purpose of being undercover, don't you think? But if we did have officers under cover, what might we have found out?'

'Well, the word in the pub is, Bob Barnes had to find ten thousand quid in a hurry or his wife would be dressing in black. Which, now, I suppose she will be.'

'Any idea who he needed the money for?'

Farrell shook his head. 'Barnes was into all sorts of stuff. I don't know who he was in trouble with. But maybe it was the people he owed the money to who killed him.'

'Well, Faz, I might find that answer attractive if I didn't know that whoever killed him also tried to kill you. And that wasn't about missing money. Was it? So, Faz, if you want protection, here's where you pay for it. Someone cut off the tip of your finger. And then they got so much heroin into you it should have killed you. Would have killed you, if some kid out there for an illicit shag hadn't heard you moan and called 999, and if the ambulancemen hadn't been carrying enough naloxone to haul you back from the brink. Who was it?'

Harry Walford watched the pair of them: Farrell upright in bed and the DI in a chair beside him, staring at each other. He might as well not have been there. It wasn't hard to understand the battle being fought in Farrell's head. On one side, a life in which he'd been taught since his earliest childhood never to tell the police anything. On the other, his wish to be guarded so that he had a chance of living beyond the next day or two.

At last, Farrell said, 'Yes, I broke into the Unity Corp building. As I said, I was looking for a book that Bob Barnes had promised me two hundred pounds for. Three men found me there. They put me in a chair and beat me up a bit to try to get me to tell them who had sent me. When I refused, they cut the tip off my finger with a pair of shears. That's when I told them I'd been sent by Bob Barnes. I don't remember anything else until I woke up in here today.'

'Thank you,' said Julie.

'I'll get a guard?'

'You've had one since the moment you came in here. Did you think we'd leave unprotected someone as vulnerable as you?' She stood up and patted him on the cheek. 'It's time you realised, Faz, that the police are your friends.'

When they got outside, Julie had Walford send a report to the HOLMES receiver, describing what had just happened. Minutes later, DCI McIntyre called her.

'Well done, Julie. You got us exactly what we needed. I'm declaring the Unity Corp building a crime scene, I'm having anyone on the premises arrested and brought in for questioning under caution and I'm sending scenes of crime in there to see what they can find. An excellent result.'

But when they got back to the station, they found out the birds had flown. DCI McIntyre said, 'It's a crime scene, and we'll find whatever forensics have been left. But there are no people and an immediate sweep suggests that any incriminating contraband –

like the heroin that nearly killed Farrell – has been removed.'

'Do we keep the security on Farrell?'

'I think we have to. And we could try putting him with a police artist to see what kind of photofit he can come up with. But I won't pretend to be optimistic. Whatever it is these people do, they are professionals. They've calculated the odds and decided it's time to move on.'

CHAPTER 19

The contrast between the beach, brightly lit by moonlight, and the darkness of the forest just beyond could, at the right time and in the right company, have been the height of romance. In fact, she was terrified. The shapes that had emerged from the trees looked like big dogs. Mary had been born and raised in Chester. Apart from the occasional alcohol-loaded week in Mallorca or Ibiza, she had never been further than Liverpool. It took a while for the word to penetrate her horrified mind, because they didn't have what she was looking at in Chester, or Liverpool, or Mallorca, or Ibiza. They weren't dogs. They were wolves. And they were looking at her. And she didn't need a degree in animal behaviour to know they were seeing dinner.

She knew nothing about wolves. Nothing about the behaviour of animals that hunt in packs. But not knowing didn't mean not understanding. There were six of them, and they had spread out into an arc. At the centre of the arc was her. And they were moving, slowly but implacably, nose to the ground, in her direction.

She picked up a stone and hurled it in the direction of the wolf at the centre of the arc. 'You throw like a girl' her brothers had told her when a girl was what she still was, but growing up with two boys had taught her something and the stone caught the wolf right on the nose. It leaped in the air and let out a scream to curdle the blood. The ring of predators moved back a foot or so. But they weren't leaving.

Mary started gathering stones that she could throw if they started their forward movement again. She collected five of about the right size. Five. If she threw them as well as the first, that might save her from the next five advances. But what would happen when they came a sixth time?

Fire was what she needed. Fire kept animals at bay. That's how early men had protected their cave dwellings from the creatures that would have eaten them. Mary knew that from watching television as a girl. The tide and storms had brought driftwood to the shore. A lot was wet – but further up toward the tree line, some looked dry and brittle enough to burn. And in her bag was a cigarette lighter and a notebook. Enough to start a fire? There was only one way to find out.

With one eye always on the wolves and a stone always in her hand, she began to pick up pieces of dry driftwood from the area nearest to her. In the time it took to heap them up and rip paper from her notebook to stuff into gaps, she used two of her five stones. The wolves had been held, but they were closer than when she had started. If this fire didn't work... Well, what was the point of thinking about that? If she couldn't get the fire going, she was as good as dead.

She pushed another piece of crumpled up paper into the pile of wood and clicked her cigarette lighter. The paper caught; a tiny flame rose... But there was no instant spread. She needed wind. And there was a little, and it did seem that it might be rising, but perhaps that was wishful thinking.

Mary hunched down and watched as the wolves, back on their feet, began to move toward her once more. She had to give it to these animals. They weren't stupid. They'd learned the lesson of the stones she had thrown and the lesson was: stones could hurt but they didn't kill. She had no idea what sense of smell wolves had, but she suspected they smelled a meal big enough to leave them asleep for hours.

They were moving faster now. Mary stood and, with every ounce of power at her disposal, hurled one of her three remaining stones at the wolf running in the centre. This was her best hit yet – she hadn't just stopped the animal; she had hurt it. The wolf rolled over onto its back and the others gathered round, howling at the sky. She'd bought herself a little time. But she'd been abandoned here with no hope of rescue and time was on the wolves' side and not on hers.

And then a gust of wind stronger than anything so far fanned the tiny flame into life. Branches around it caught, and soon the whole pile of wood she had gathered was on fire. What she needed now was to keep it going. She gathered more wood, choosing thicker pieces and what amounted to logs which would burn for longer once they caught.

She looked across the fire toward the wolves. They had moved back. Only a little, and they weren't going away, but nor did it look as though they were going to advance any further as long as the fire was in their way. What she needed now was to keep it burning for as long as it would take for someone to find her. Perhaps hikers in the morning passing on the trail that Max had told her stretched all the way to San Josef Bay.

If, that is, Max had been telling the truth. And even if he had, how often did people walk that trail? And what sort of people would they be? For a city dweller like Mary, it was almost impossible to imagine that anyone could undertake such a walk for pleasure.

But there was no time to worry about that now. She began to collect as much wood as she could. There'd be no sleep tonight. She recovered the clothes she'd taken off and held them close to the fire. She might not be able to sleep, but at least she could be fully dressed.

CHAPTER 20

Barry Fitzgibbon had never visited his brother since his conviction, even when he had been in a local prison. He didn't have time now to go as far as Exeter. Unless he went by helicopter. He was no stranger to helicopters – he rented one every year to go to Cheltenham races. But that was PR – this time he was doing it for convenience.

Marie said, 'You'll be there in time to see him at two this afternoon and you can be back home for dinner. I'll let you know when they are here to pick you up. Although you won't need that – you'll hear them.'

***

Claire was still with Gene Cohen when the call came from the reporter. 'Have you seen your story in our paper?'

'Not yet.'

'It's getting good coverage. TV picked it up and a little flotilla of boats has set off from Victoria, all wanting to be the first to find Mary and bring her safely home.'

'Good heavens! I hope they succeed.'

'There's more. We put Mary's picture at the top of the story. A taxi driver has rung in to say he picked her up yesterday and delivered her to a West Victoria address. You want the driver's phone number?'

Claire made a note of it. When she'd hung up, she repeated what she'd just been told to Gene Cohen. Then she called the taxi driver. This time, when she closed the call she said, 'Isn't that interesting? The address the taxi driver delivered Mary to is the one where, yesterday, they told me that Mary had never been there. I need to go back and ask why they lied.'

Cohen's expression was unreadable. 'Is that a good idea? They sound dangerous.'

'I'll be prepared. And danger is part of the job, don't you think?'

'Of course it is. But the nature of danger varies from place to place. I don't suppose, for example, the British PI carries a gun?'

Claire shook her head. 'I'd have to jump through all kinds of hoops to get a licence. And even if I had one, I couldn't carry it with me. I'd have to keep it in a locked gun cabinet.'

'We do things a little differently over here. Why don't you let me check this out?'

'Sure. But I should come with you.'

'Do you mind if we don't do that right at the start? They've seen you before – I don't want them put off before I've even spoken to them. After I've found out what they have to say, if it's necessary to go back, you could come then by all means.'

Claire thought about that. She wasn't happy to let someone else handle such a major part of the enquiry without her being present. On the other hand, she needed to get upstairs and check the email that Ted Hughes said he'd sent her. She had tried looking at it on her phone, but the phone was neither expensive nor state-of-the-art, the screen was very small, and the email looked long and easier to read on her laptop. And just at that point her phone vibrated to say someone was calling her. She answered.

'Claire? Dewi Morgan here. Have you got a minute?'

That made up her mind for her. Gene Cohen was, after all, a fellow professional and they were both being paid by Jim Fitzgibbon. She said, 'Dewi, I'll call you back in five. Okay?' Then to Cohen she said, 'Let me know what happens. And never mind the danger to me – you're the one who's going there. Stay safe. Don't take any chances.'

***

Laszlo said to Holly Evans, 'Bob Barnes is dead. Somebody killed him.'

'I heard.'

'We haven't had this week's money.'

'I know.'

'You want me to visit his wife when the police have left? Get it from her?'

'No, Laszlo. Forget it. Who knows what sort of state she'll be in? Going after her could bring the police down on our heads after everything we've done to avoid their attention. We have enough reserves to write off ten thousand. The important thing now is to find a new place to wash our money.'

'You're not afraid that word will get round? That other people will think it's all right to take our money and not give it back?'

'Laszlo. How many people do you think know that Barnes handled our money? If someone else rips us off, we'll deal with the case on its merits. That's how you stay out of trouble.'

***

After sending his email to Claire and then texting to tell her to read it, Ted Hughes had driven to a supermarket on the edge of the Chester ring road. Before starting his tour of the aisles, he bought a scone and a cup of coffee in the supermarket's café and sat down to read a newspaper that someone had left at a table. He'd been there two minutes when someone sat beside him, an expectant look on his face. It took Hughes a moment to drag from his memory the name attached to that face. He said, 'Terry Findlay. Chester's master burglar.'

Findlay raised a finger. 'Now, now, Ted. That's the sort of friendly joshing remark that can get someone a bad name.'

'How do you get away with it, Terry?'

'If I knew what you were talking about, which of course I don't, I would say that the secret might include not taking on stupid jobs.'

'Why do I get the feeling that that's why you're sitting beside me? Is there something you think I should know?'

Findlay said, 'What would be the point, Ted? You're retired.' Hughes waited; he had the sense there was more coming. He was not someone Terry Findlay normally stopped to chat to with no reason. And then Findlay said, 'Did you hear about Faz?' When Hughes shook his head, Findlay went on, 'You really are retired. There was a time when someone would have given you a ring. Information in return for a fiver. Though I imagine the rate has gone up a little since your day.'

'I wouldn't know, Terry. I'm not in the market for information any more. But tell me about Glenn Farrell.'

'Poor old Faz. Word is, he's in the Countess of Chester. Word also is, he's damn lucky to be alive. The heaviest heroin overdose they've ever seen is what I heard.'

'What was it? Unusually pure?'

'Faz isn't a user, Ted. The way I hear it, this dose was not self-administered. The other thing I hear is that he got it when he was caught trying to burgle Unity Corp.'

Ted Hughes saw the sudden excitement in Findlay's eyes. It was something he'd seen many times before during his working career and he knew what it meant: whoever was speaking to him had reached the point where he was ready to hand over information a crime correspondent could use to his advantage. He waited.

'Thing is, Ted, a couple of days ago I had the strangest conversation with Bob Barnes about Unity Corp.'

'Bob Barnes? At the Moor's Head?'

'Is there some other Bob Barnes? Well, I suppose there must be, but I don't know him. Anyway, Bob Barnes made the strangest request. I don't know where he can have got the idea, but he asked me to burgle Unity Corp. Me!'

Hughes shook his head. 'Incredible. A law-abiding gent like you, never did a wrong thing in his life, wouldn't even know how to start burgling somewhere, and right out of nowhere someone asks you to do it. I can scarcely believe it. What did you say?'

'The obvious, of course. That I'm not a burglar and so I'm not going to break into Unity Corp. I also told him, though, that even if I had been a burglar...'

'As if...' Hughes smiled.

'...I still wouldn't break into Unity Corp. I said you'd have to be insane. Which, of course, I am not. But he was desperate. Word is, he owed ten thousand quid to someone you don't want to owe money to. Word is, he'd asked his brother-in-law Barry for a loan. And Fitzgibbon refused. But he said, if Barnes would arrange for someone to steal something Fitzgibbon wanted from Unity Corp, then Fitzgibbon wouldn't just lend him the ten grand. He'd make him a present of it.'

'I see. And you are telling me this because... Why? Surely, an upstanding, law-abiding citizen like you should be sharing this information with CID?'

'Problems with that, Ted. Collaborating with the law doesn't come easy to someone like me. I could maybe overcome that, but who in CID could I trust with the info? Barry Fitzgibbon is involved here, and Barry is not a man who forgives. I know Cedric Walters was caught and did his time, but who's to say Walters was the only bad apple in that barrel? On the whole, it seems unlikely. And it only needs one bent copper to whisper in Barry Fitzgibbon's ear, and I might find myself needing to leave Chester in a hurry. And I like it here.'

'So you'd like me to do it?'

'Me? Ted, all I'm doing is shooting the breeze with an old mate. If I happen to give the old mate information, what the old mate does with it is his business. As long as he doesn't mention my name, of course.'

Ted had finished his scone and realised that he'd let his coffee go cold. He pushed it away and stood up. 'Well, thank you. I'll give what you've told me some thought.'

'I can ask no more.'

***

Claire went back to her room and phoned Dewi, who told her that Bert Musk had wanted to see her but that when he'd gone to the care home, Musk had been in a bad place, mentally. 'I don't know what he wanted to tell us, but whatever it was, we are going to have to wait. I'll call every day to see if he's in a state to talk to me. What he said to Rio Wood, the carer, suggests he has something on his mind.'

'Thanks, Dewi. Keep in touch.'

Then at last she was able to read the email from Ted Hughes. She sat immobile as the meaning of one sentence unwrapped itself in her mind. Gene Cohen was not the stranger to this case that he had pretended to be. Gene Cohen had been involved from the start. And he was the man she had allowed to go on her behalf to ask Miriam Donovan why she had lied. The man to whom she had given the coordinates of the tracker she had got the unknowing Mary Barnes to carry in her bag.

He was more than that. He was the investigator in whom Marie had told her Barry Fitzgibbon had complete confidence.

What had Cohen done to earn that trust?

CHAPTER 21

When Julie Roberts and Harry Walford arrived at the car dealership owned by Barry Fitzgibbon, Marie told them he wasn't there.

Julie said, 'May I ask where he is?'

'He's in Exeter. Visiting his brother in prison. He went by helicopter. He should be back later today. Can I help?'

'Mr Fitzgibbon's name has come up in connection with a matter we are investigating. We need to speak to him.'

'I'll let him know.'

Harry said, 'We'd also like to talk to Mr Fitzgibbon's sister. Do you have any idea where she might be?'

'Mary Barnes? I believe she's in Canada.'

'Canada? Is she on holiday?'

Marie gave him a look that suggested he should have a better grip of police business. 'I don't know all the details, but I understand that she came to talk to you people about something to do with her brother. The one Mr Fitzgibbon is visiting in Exeter. Nothing came of that, and so she decided to go to Canada and investigate it for herself.'

'When did she go?' asked Julie.

'Three days ago? Four? I can't be sure.'

'So she may not know her husband has been murdered.'

For the first time, Marie showed signs of being flustered. 'Murdered? I didn't know myself. I'm not sure Mr Fitzgibbon is aware.'

Julie said, 'We issued a press report. It was in the paper this morning.'

'We get the local paper here, of course. We are a major advertiser. I don't think anyone reads it for news.'

'We need to speak to Mr Fitzgibbon as soon as possible.'

'I'll see that he knows that.'

***

About an hour after he'd dropped Mary, Max pulled into Port Hardy. He'd refuel here, get something to eat and sleep a while. But reaching harbour brought him back into satellite phone reception and his wife had been calling him every fifteen minutes ever since Dane had reached home. 'Go back and pick her up, Max.'

'Dane's talked to you.'

'Of course he has. He doesn't want to see you in trouble any more than I do. But I will, Max, if anything happens to that woman.'

'I don't have a choice. Miriam…'

'Yes, Max, I know about the hold Miriam has over you. But I've got one, too.'

'You? What are you talking about?'

'Oh, Max. Do you think I never knew what you'd been up to before we met? Think of all the people who knew you. People who, since we married, also know me. And all Miriam has is rumour. She can tell the police you were there, but she can't prove it. I, on the other hand, have evidence.'

Max breathed out. He couldn't believe... But... 'Have you been looking through my stuff?'

'You should have got rid of it, Max. A gun that killed someone. You should have dropped it overboard a mile offshore. Why on earth did you keep it? But you did.'

'You wouldn't...'

'Max. You'd better believe I would. I've been so proud of you, the way you made something of your life after a start like that, the father you've been to Dane, the husband you've been to me. But love and loyalty have their limits. I'm not standing by while you kill someone. This woman you kidnapped is all over the papers. And the television. You bring her safely home, or I'll turn you in. And then they'll have you for two murders instead of one.'

'Julie. It's been more than an hour. She could be dead already.'

'You'd better hope she isn't. Midday, Max. That's the deadline. If her photograph isn't all over the TV by then, and if I can't see that she's living and breathing, you'll be spending the rest of your life behind bars.'

'But…'

'Midday, Max. Don't ask for an extension. There won't be one.'

***

Barry Fitzgibbon got Marie's text message just before he went into the visiting room. He wasn't allowed to take his phone into the room itself, so he started to tell Jim what was in it, but Jim interrupted him.

'Visitors normally buy me a coffee.' He gestured with his head toward a counter, behind which three women were serving non-alcoholic drinks and confectionery. 'And a KitKat would be nice. I like the dark chocolate ones.'

Barry went to the counter and came back with the requested items. 'Get many visitors?'

'Tom comes every few months. Nobody else. Not since they moved me down here. Mary came a few times when I was closer. She writes to me, too, from time to time. And Tom sends me a Father's Day card.'

'He knows, then?'

'That I'm his father? He seems to have worked it out. Of course, he's had the benefit of an expensive education. I gather I have you to thank for that.'

Barry shrugged. 'Matter of interest, why did they move you down here? It's miles from anywhere.'

'I was Category A for years. They'd like to see the back of me now but they can't put me in a Category C prison because they'd be embarrassed if I escaped without being released. Exeter is Category B.'

'If they want you gone, why don't they just kick you out?'

'I have to say I'm sorry before they'll do that. And that would mean admitting I killed her. Which I didn't.' He paused, his eyes resting on his brother. 'As I think you know.'

'Wouldn't it be worth saying you did? To get out?'

'I can see how people might think that. You wouldn't like to buy me another KitKat would you?' When Barry had brought the chocolate bar to the table, Jim said, 'So that's my visiting list. My son two or three times a year and my sister once in a blue moon. But never my brother. Never you. Why are you here now? What is it you want?'

'Did you know Mary has gone to Canada?'

Jim shook his head. 'Should I?'

'I don't mean on holiday. She's gone to investigate a woman she thinks is Sally Varney.'

Jim finished his coffee and ate the last of his KitKat. 'Sally. After all this time. What do you know? I never believed she was dead.'

'If she isn't, she's dangerous.'

'I guess.'

'Mary took ten thousand quid from Bob to get there.'

'Naughty.'

'Bob was washing it for someone. And now he's dead.'

Jim nodded. 'Well, the kind of people who need that sort of money cleaned up... You don't want to cross them.'

'You knew nothing about this?'

'How would I? I haven't talked to Mary in months.'

'I paid a private investigator to follow Mary to Canada and watch her back.'

'That was generous.'

'She's my sister as well as yours.'

'Of course.' He rolled the silver paper from his second KitKat into a little ball. 'It was a pyramid, wasn't it? Your diamond thing. A Ponzi.'

'What are you talking about? Anything I've been involved in was straight.'

'Who knew about it? That's what I've wondered.'

'Oh, you have, have you? Is that what you do? Stuck in places like this for thirty-odd years? You wonder about your brother's business?'

'What else do I have to do? See, that's how it goes when you're doing life. You have lots of time to sit and think. Somebody stuck it to you and here you are, doing time for someone else's crime. But whose? And you think, day after day, and bit by bit you start to see a picture. Just a possible picture, you understand – nothing you can prove. But a picture that makes sense when nothing else does.'

'Jim...'

'A business like that, it would need records. And if anyone got their hands on those records... Well. They'd have the seller by the balls. Wouldn't they?'

'Jim...'

'So that's the kind of thinking you do when you're banged up in here with nothing to do and you've read every book in the prison library at least twice and you've never been the biggest reader anyway . And then you get to thinking, what would I do if I was the one selling the diamonds and those books were mine and someone had got hold of them and was putting the squeeze on me? And what would someone else do? Someone maybe that little bit more determined than me. That touch more ruthless.'

'That's what you think about, is it?'

Jim nodded. 'Plenty of time for thinking in prison, Barry.'

'Well, brother of mine, here's something else to think about. If you ever do get out of here, you're going to need someone to take care of you. Otherwise it won't be long before you're sheltering from the elements in a cardboard box under a bridge somewhere. And the only person I can think of who might have the money to take care of you is me. So you might want to be a bit careful about some of this thinking you do. And even more careful about who you talk to on the subject.' He stood up. 'I think we're done here.'

'Me too, Barry. Thanks for coming. Maybe do it again in another thirty years.'

Barry turned toward a prison officer, raised an eyebrow and pointed toward the exit. The officer nodded, walked over to the table and led Barry to the door, unlocking and opening it for him. Barry turned back for a last look at his brother. The visit had been a mistake.

***

The fire had kept the wolves at bay, but now it was burning down and Mary faced her next problem. All of the dry wood near enough to collect without getting too far from the fire had now been burned. She needed more. And there was more – a lot of it. But between it and her were the wolves.

The wolves were closer now. They could see the fire wasn't as big as it had been. She wondered what it was like to be a wolf. They'd have to take their food where they found it. And sometimes it would be a bigger animal than one wolf could manage on its own. This was Canada – didn't they have elk and moose here? If you were a wolf and you lived like that, you'd learn patience. Wouldn't you?

For the first time, the thought began to take root in her mind: she wasn't going to survive this night. But she wasn't going down without a fight.

***

Claire's phone gave the kind of ring that said someone was making a video call on WhatsApp. She looked at the name: Ted Hughes. She swiped up. 'Ted! A man your age! WhatsApp! I'm impressed.'

'My granddaughters keep me up-to-date. You've read my email?'

'I have. And I've got some bad news. Barry Fitzgibbon hired a Canadian investigator to give me a hand here. An investigator he'd had dealings with before. The investigator's name is Eugene Cohen.'

Hughes was silent for a few moments. Then he said, 'It's going to take a while for what that means to sink in. But I suggest you need to be even more careful than you were already being. I don't know whether you've heard this from someone else but, if not, Mary Barnes is a widow. Her husband was killed. Somewhat brutally, from what I hear. Will you tell her?'

'I can't. She's missing. And I'm pretty sure she was abducted when she went to visit the woman she thinks is Sally Varney.'

'Does Barry know that?'

'Yes, he does. And right after I told him, he put Gene Cohen on the job.'

'Interesting. You don't think you should come home now? Before something happens to you?'

'Not just yet. I took on the job of watching Mary Barnes's back and I've been paid for it. I'm not going home until I know what's happened to her.'

'Okay. But watch your step. It sounds like you're mixing with people who don't much care who gets hurt as long as it isn't them. Hey, let me tell you about the conversation I had at Sainsbury's with Terry Findlay.'

When he'd done that, Claire said, 'So Terry Findlay wants you to tell the police that Bob Barnes hired an incompetent burglar because he desperately needed ten thousand quid and it got him killed. Which, if true, means Mary signed his death warrant when she took that money. Will you do what he wants?'

'Tell the cops? I might tell Tina Howard first. There could be the makings of a great story there. She can't run it, of course, not just as it is, but if she is the one who tells the cops she may get herself some brownie points. A head start with the story when the police are ready to let it go live.'

'Good idea. And thanks for not bringing up the time I failed to follow an idea every bit as good.'

Hughes laughed. 'I figure you think about that often enough as it is. Gotta go now – if I hear any more, I'll be in touch.'

Claire opened a bottle of water and took a chocolate bar from the room's fridge. No doubt the cost would be excessive but the one who'd be paying it had grievously misled her. She thought about the conversation she'd just had with Ted Hughes and the way it had ended. Was he right? Did she often think about the misjudgement that had ended her journalistic career?

Yes he was, and yes she did.

She'd felt, in that courtroom, like a naughty girl back in school sent to stand on the naughty step. The judge was a woman old enough to be Claire's mother, but sympathetic in a way Claire's mother had never been. She said, 'I realise that you did not intend to break the law. I understand that your intention was to write the best story you could and you may have been a little carried away. And, of course, the story you wrote didn't get into print because your editor knew better than to let that happen. But in conducting your interviews you gave people suspected of criminal intent information they should not have had. You made public details of a case that the police wished to remain confidential until the matter had been aired in court. When you did that, you jeopardised a trial concerning a very serious crime, and that is contempt of court. Because of your actions, an accused person walked free. We will never know whether that was the right outcome because the charges can never now be put to the accused in front of a jury. This is not America. There exists in this country a newspaper code of conduct in reporting criminal proceedings and you broke it. Your counsel has put forward in mitigation the fact that you lost your job as a result and are now unlikely ever to work in journalism again. That being the case, I am not going to impose a custodial sentence, but please do not interpret that as in any way reducing the seriousness of your offence.'

Claire could call those words to mind any time she wished and frequently when she did not. The look on the judge's face was one she would never forget.

CHAPTER 22

Max was about a mile from the place where he'd left Mary Barnes. He turned the wheel to bring the Bayliner closer to the shore. He sniffed the air. Fire. Maybe Mary had lit it. Maybe someone else did, but if so she might have found them. And then he saw the flame. He grabbed the binoculars from under his seat and focused on the area where he'd seen flashes of light. It was Mary. She was still alive. But she wasn't alone. He'd have given anything for a rifle, but even if he'd had one there would have been questions to answer because this was a national park and wolves were a protected species. He needed to distract them.

There were flares in the emergency storage, but he needed to be closer, and speeding up was out of the question this close to shore. There were too many submerged obstacles. Max drowning wouldn't help Mary.

***

Tina Howard thanked Ted Hughes for the story he had given her. 'The moment I've given it to the police I'll be around at yours with a bottle of Famous Grouse.'

'Much appreciated, Tina. Did you know Claire Tanner smokes Marlboro?'

'What? You want me to bring you a carton?'

'I was thinking of a pack. A carton would be too generous. But don't let that stop you.'

Tina rang DI Julie Roberts. 'I have a story I'd like to tell you. I can't use it in the paper, for reasons you'll understand when you've heard it, but I think you might find it very useful.'

'It's nice of you to call, Tina, but the Press Office is how we communicate with the media. Perhaps you should be talking to them.'

'I don't think so, Inspector. The Press Office is for when you tell us things. Or when you don't tell us things but you want to look as though you are. And this is me telling you things.'

'Okay. I have ten minutes. Can you get here now?'

And Julie was glad she'd made that arrangement because, when Barry Fitzgibbon called half an hour later to say he was back from Exeter and available to speak to the police, she was holding a little more ammunition than she would have been if she hadn't spoken to Tina first. Not that she expected to get anything out of Fitzgibbon. He was too experienced a hand.

'Mr Fitzgibbon. I understand you've been to visit your brother?'

Barry nodded. 'Naturally, it's a grievance to us as a family to have someone so close serving a prison sentence for such a serious offence. I don't mind telling you, I hold him responsible for our mother dying years before her time. She was heartbroken that a Fitzgibbon should have brought such harm to the family's name. Nevertheless, family is family and he is my brother.'

Julie, who had read the Fitzgibbon file and knew how many times the family's name had been besmirched by the man Fitzgibbon's mother had been married to and by other Fitzgibbons, smiled. 'I'm sure your mother must have been deeply hurt. And now we have the death of your brother-in-law, Bob Barnes.'

Barry's face gave every sign of a shocked man ready to mourn. 'I knew nothing about that until Marie – that's my PA – told me. What on earth happened to Bob?'

'We've issued a press release, Mr Fitzgibbon. You can read in the newspaper everything we want to say at this moment. And the Moor's Head is still a crime scene. We are examining everything of interest there.' She watched Fitzgibbon's face closely, but he gave no sign of concern about what she had just said. Whatever SOCO found in the pub, it was unlikely to incriminate Barry Fitzgibbon. She said, 'We haven't as yet been able to speak to Mrs Barnes. She may not know that her husband is dead.'

'No. When Marie told me about poor Bob's passing, I tried calling my sister. She didn't answer, and so I thought of texting her. But, honestly – is that the way she would want to receive such sad information?'

'Do you happen to know where she is?'

'Yes. She's in Canada.'

That was a shame. She would have preferred it if he had denied knowing about Mary Barnes's whereabouts so that she could confront him with the fact that not only did he know where Mary was but had also sent someone after her. That was the problem with intelligent suspects; they were bright enough always to tell the truth unless the truth was impossibly damaging to them. If Julie was honest with herself, most of the convictions they got came when people less bright than Fitzgibbon incriminated themselves. She didn't think he was likely to do that. Still, it was always worth a try. She said, 'Is she on holiday there?'

Fitzgibbon smiled. Julie didn't like the smile one little bit. It said 'I know you know why she's there. And now you know I know you know. But by all means, let's play your game.' And the smile was replaced with a look of earnest collaboration. 'No, she isn't, Inspector. As you may know, although it happened long before your time, my brother Jim is serving a life sentence for murdering a woman called Sally Varney. My sister uncovered evidence that Sally Varney may still be alive and living in Canada. Which, if true, would raise serious concerns about the enquiry the police conducted more than thirty years ago and the evidence they put before the court. In any case, Mary took the evidence she believed she had to you, you put no credence in it, and she went to Canada in an attempt to prove you wrong.'

'Do you know how she paid for the trip?'

'Yes, I'm afraid I do. She took money Bob was planning to deposit in the bank. And I'm afraid the money did not belong to Bob. If he's been killed, you need to talk to the people whose money it was. I can't help you there – I have no idea who they were.'

Dammit. Almost the last shot in her locker and it had hit nothing. 'How do you know it wasn't her husband's money?'

'Because he told me. He said he'd be in serious trouble if he didn't find the money, and he asked me to lend it to him. I'm afraid I refused. If I'd known it was going to get him killed, I might have taken a different line. But perhaps not... It was obvious that the money he had been looking after came from criminal activity and my fear was that, if I helped him out, I'd somehow become an accomplice.' He held his hands out in a gesture of ignorance. 'I'm just an honest businessman... I know nothing about how these things are done. And I wasn't very happy to know that my sister's husband had involved her in wrongdoing, even if she knew nothing about it.'

'An attempt was also made on the life of Glenn Farrell.'

'Farrell? I'm sorry, I'm afraid I don't recognise the name.'

'He is an habitual burglar.'

'He is? And you think this... What did you call it? This attempt on his life was connected with Bob's death?'

'Mr Farrell has told us that your brother-in-law hired him to break into premises occupied by a company called Unity Corp and find a book.'

'Unity Corp – I don't know them. What do they do?'

'The suggestion has been made that the book was for you.'

'Me! What would I want with a book? I'm not the world's greatest reader, Inspector.'

The suggestion was that you would pay Bob Barnes the ten thousand pounds he needed in return for that book.'

'What? This Farrell man said that?'

'No. That suggestion came from elsewhere.'

'Well, Inspector, I hope you're treating it with contempt. Because that is what it deserves. Bob Barnes asked me to lend him ten thousand pounds. I refused. And I've heard no more about the subject. Now... Is there anything else? Because here to Exeter and back is a long trip, even by helicopter. I had no lunch, and I'd like to go home and get something to eat.'

When he had gone, Harry Walford said, 'What did you make of all that?'

'He was laughing at us. He knows why Bob Barnes was killed. In all likelihood, he knows who killed him. Does he care? He does not. Can we pin it on him? Not a chance.'

'So we do nothing?'

'I'll tell you what... It might be time to dust off the murder Jim Fitzgibbon was jailed for and take another look at it. But we won't get Sylvie McIntyre's agreement to that until the Bob Barnes murder and Glenn Farrell's attempted murder have been wrapped up. So let's go and find out what our next job on HOLMES is.'

CHAPTER 23

They were getting closer. Mary took the long length of tree branch she'd been holding back and held it in the fire, waiting for the end to catch. They might be about to make her their meal for that night, but she'd burn at least one of the horrible grey bastards before they got her.

And then a burst of red smoke flew over her head and crashed among the wolves, which scattered and ran with a cacophony of canine screams, and she heard a voice behind her. 'Mary! Here! Run!'

And she turned, and she saw the boat that had brought her here bobbing as close to the shore as Max dared take it, and she picked up her bag and she ran.

When she reached the Bayliner, Max grabbed her and hauled her on board. And the fear and the horror she'd been holding at bay overwhelmed her, tossing her around like a leaf passing over Niagara Falls on the other side of this continent. She sat in the back of the boat, sobbing her heart out as Max headed back into deep water after handing her a chocolate bar and a cup of coffee. She took one last look back at the shore. The wolves had regrouped and were standing at the water's edge, howling and looking out to sea.

Looking at her.

***

Claire looked at her phone. The tracker, which had been stationary so long at the northern tip of Vancouver Island, had begun to move. She thought of ringing Gene Cohen to ask for his input. And then she thought again. Gene Cohen was not to be trusted. She could let Barry Fitzgibbon know, but Barry Fitzgibbon would tell Gene Cohen. And then she realised that there was no point worrying about this, because Gene Cohen had the tracker's coordinates and he could see that the tracker was moving as well as she could.

Rule those calls out and there was nothing Claire could do until the tracker came to a halt and she could investigate whether Mary was with it. Instead, she checked her watch. It was two hours after midnight here, but in England it would be seven in the evening. A good time to tell her sister she hoped to be home soon and check out how she was. She dialled Daisy's number.

***

When Julie Roberts told the Major Investigation Team's evening briefing session about her conversations with Tina Howard and then with Barry Fitzgibbon, DCI McIntyre said, 'Did you promise the reporter anything?'

'Nothing, boss. She asked for a head start when we have any news to release and I said that was a matter for the Press Office.'

'And so it is. Still, there can't be any harm in doing her a favour. It's always good to have the local press on your side. God knows they give us a hard enough time when they feel like it.

'Right. Let's talk about where we go next. There are two main lines of enquiry into the death of Bob Barnes. One is the people, whoever they are, that he owed ten thousand quid to. We can take it that he really did owe ten thousand pounds because we have it from more than one source. So that is something that needs to be established: who did Bob Barnes launder money for, assuming that it was a regular thing? And a regular thing it does seem to have been. But the other is Unity Corp. SOCO have turned their building over and we have some promising DNA and fingerprint leads. We also have evidence that significant amounts of proscribed drugs have been held there until very recently. We know that Glenn Farrell was drugged to the eyeballs, in an attempt to kill him, by men who found him inside the Unity Corp building, and we know that there were strong similarities between the treatment given to

Farrell and the later murder of Bob Barnes. That's enough to assume, for the moment, that people from Unity Corp murdered Bob Barnes. What we don't know is whether Barnes's money laundering was also for Unity Corp.'

Julie Roberts said, 'You think it might not have been? Isn't that a bit of a coincidence? That Bob Barnes gets into trouble with two sets of people at the same time?'

McIntyre looked around. 'This is the moment when someone says Occam's razor.' When she saw only blank faces looking back at her, she said, 'That's the theory that the simplest solution is always the right one. And it's true that the simplest solution – the one that combines all possible offenders in one neat little package – is that Unity Corp gave money every week to Bob Barnes to launder for them and that, when he didn't have the money to give back to them, they killed him. So that is a central line of investigation that we will continue to follow. But it isn't the only one. For starters, it doesn't explain why Unity Corp would also try to murder Glenn Farrell. It's also possible that Barnes laundered money for someone else. That he got Farrell to try to find whatever it was that Barry Fitzgibbon wanted from the Unity Corp building so that Fitzgibbon would give him the money to pay off whoever the someone else was, and that Farrell gave up Fitzgibbon's name when Unity Corp tortured him. Which is certainly what Farrell says. Any ideas?'

A detective sergeant held up his hand.

'Yes, Barney,' said McIntyre.

'Why would Bob Barnes choose Farrell to burgle the Unity Corp building?'

'Not sure I follow, Barney.'

'You'd be hard pressed to find a more incompetent burglar than Farrell within a hundred miles of Chester. A number of more useful robbers and safe-crackers drink in the Moor's Head. Bob Barnes knows them. So why choose Faz?'

'What can we do with that idea, Barney?'

'We need to talk to some of the others. Did Barnes pitch the idea to them before he took it to Farrell? Is there anything else they can tell us?'

McIntyre looked at Julie. 'Worth a shot,' said Julie. 'Good thinking, Barney.'

McIntyre turned to the HOLMES receiver. 'Put three detective constables on that. Have them report to Barney. Any other suggestions?'

Detective Sergeant Sally Fortune raised her hand. 'Barnes had a separate paying-in book for the money he laundered through the bank. Our task,' – and she indicated the detective constable beside her – 'was to find out what happened to that money.'

'And you have?'

'It took a lot of unpicking. They didn't set out to make things easy. And, of course, the bank did everything it could to get in our way. But in the end the picture is clear. There were regular transfers to a bank in Hereford. The account the money went to there is in the name of Holly Holdings, which is a trading name for a woman called Holly Evans. But Holly Evans doesn't live in Hereford – she lives in Ruthin. We asked North Wales Police what they could tell us about Holly Evans and the answer was, not a lot. She's never been in trouble. She's suspected of no crimes. She lives on her own in a large house on the outskirts that they reckon would run you more than half a million pounds, which puts it at the high-end for Ruthin. She drives a top of the range Lexus LC Convertible, and when she goes on holiday she flies in the front of the plane and stays at the most expensive hotels. And she doesn't appear to have any job at all.'

'That doesn't sound like not a lot – that's prime information.'

'As far as it goes, sure – but what about the questions it doesn't answer? What does she live on? If she hasn't got a job, how does she pay for the car and the holidays? North Wales Police say they can put a forensic accounting team on the job, but we would have to pay for it. Or, they say, we can do it ourselves. They won't raise any objection to our carrying out a forensic investigation on their patch.'

'We could, of course, get her in here and ask her to explain where the money comes from. But she's probably got an answer ready for that. So it would be better if we had at least some idea of what she gets up to. I'd have trouble getting the budget for a team from another force. Especially as they'd no doubt pad the invoices. So we'd better do it ourselves. Do you feel competent to head that up?'

'Sure. If I can have input from the forensic accounting team here.'

'I'll have to speak to the superintendent, but you can take it for granted that you have that.' She turned again to the HOLMES receiver. 'Log that as a job for Sally Fortune. Right, I think that's it, so let's all go home, get a good night's rest and be ready to start again in the morning.'

CHAPTER 24

In the back of the Bayliner, Mary was almost catatonic. Max said, 'I wasn't going to come back for you.' Mary stared at him. She might have been taking in what he said and she might not. He couldn't tell. 'I can't explain now what I thought I was doing. I expected you to die and I was ready to let that happen because my sister asked me to. Fortunately for you, my son saw things differently. I'm not going to put you back ashore. We'll stop at Port Hardy because I'm almost out of chocolate bars and I need breakfast. And then I'll take you back to Victoria. You have a hotel there?' He was pretty sure she nodded. He might have been wrong – it wasn't much of a nod – but he thought she was taking in what he said. 'I'll take you to it. You're not going to be harmed. But I don't want my sister harmed, either. I think she may have got herself involved with someone she shouldn't be involved with. But she is involved and she is my sister and I care about her. So I need you to tell me why they wanted you dead.'

It took Mary so long to speak that he was sure it wasn't going to happen. Then she said, 'The woman who lives with your sister.'

'Yes? Ellen?'

'Her name isn't Ellen. She is Sally Varney.'

'Who?'

'Thirty-two years ago, my brother was sentenced to life imprisonment for killing Sally Varney. He is still inside. He's always denied killing her. And he's been telling the truth. Because Sally Varney is calling herself Ellen and living with your sister.'

Max remained silent for a long time. Then he said, 'You're certain about this?'

'I was pretty sure before I knocked on their door. But now I'm certain. Why else would they want me dead?'

Max could see no sensible answer to that. He said, 'Okay. She wanted you dead. But you aren't dead, and you owe that to me. So the question is, what are you going to do for me in return?'

Exhausted as she was, Mary shifted position to look at him. 'What do you want me to do?'

'Go home. Say nothing to anyone. Now or ever. Get on with the rest of your life and let my sister and her partner get on with theirs.'

Now it was Mary's turn to be silent. At last she said, 'And what about my brother?'

'I can't help your brother.'

There was another long pause. 'I'll think about it. But I need to sleep.'

When she had drifted away, Max called his wife and told her about the conversation he'd just had. He said, 'I think that's the best I'm going to get. And she could promise anything right now and it might not mean a thing. She could promise, just to make sure I let her go, and then she could sing her heart out.'

'But she's alive, Max. Which means you did the right thing.'

As he drove on, the sun began to rise. As far as he could see was bathed in golden light. He said, 'I'm going to want the most enormous breakfast when we get to Port Hardy.' But he was speaking to himself because Mary was still completely out of it.

***

Gene Cohen waited till six the next morning before ringing the Donovan's doorbell. That didn't prevent Miriam from telling him it was too early to be answering the door. He said, 'Let me in. I need to talk to you.'

'What's happened?'

'The investigator from England who came to see you? What did you tell your brother? What instructions did you give him?'

'I told him we needed to be rid of this woman.'

'Permanently? You told him to kill her?'

'Not in precisely those words. But he won't have been in any doubt that's what we wanted. Why are you asking? What's going on?'

'Would you expect him to do it?'

'Max? Yes. I wouldn't have entrusted it to him otherwise. What's all this about?'

'He'd go to jail for you? I've heard of brotherly love, but nothing on this scale. Is he retarded?'

'He got away with something when he was young. Something that could have landed him in jail for a long time and still could. I covered for him. If I got a fit of conscience... But he won't go to jail for freeing the world of Mary Barnes. No-one knows he took her away from here. They don't have licence-plate-recognition cameras at sea. No-one's been filming him.'

'The tracker stayed where it was for a few hours. Now it's moving again. My guess is, it's heading for Port Hardy.'

'So? He's left the body and he's taken her purse. He wants to dump it as far from the body as he can. He's using his brain.'

'I hope you're right. But I think we need to be watching the news for the next few hours. It may become necessary to get you and Ellen out of here in a hurry.'

'You worry too much. You want to stay for breakfast?'

CHAPTER 25

Miriam and Ellen Donovan were vegans and the breakfast they gave Gene Cohen was a vegan breakfast. Some distance away in Port Hardy, Max Donovan was tucking into two fried eggs with sausages, ranch fries, bacon, pancakes and maple syrup. Mary had asked for two slices of toast and two rashers of bacon and made herself a bacon sandwich. Neither of them had seen yesterday evening's newspaper, and they were so engaged in the food in front of them that they failed to notice the waitress and the short-order cook comparing a photograph in the newspaper with the woman they had just served. After a short conversation, the waitress put down the newspaper, moved out of sight of the dining room, and called the RCMP.

A few minutes later, a marked car drove into the parking lot and a man and woman in uniform got out and went into the diner. The waitress pointed them toward the table.

'Mary Barnes?' asked the male Mountie.

Mary stared at him, while Max stared at Mary. 'I'm sorry?'

'Ma'am, are you Mary Barnes from Chester in the UK?'

'I... Yes. I'm Mary.'

'Ma'am, would you mind telling me where you've been since yesterday?'

'I'm sorry?'

The female Mountie handed Mary a copy of the previous day's newspaper. 'This might make my colleague's question clear.'

Mary read the story. She made the paper available for Max to read it, too. Then she said, 'Oh, my. I have caused trouble. I'm so sorry.' When the two Mounties looked at her without comment, she said, 'I came over here because I thought I'd identified someone from more than thirty years ago by looking at a photograph on social media. Of course, that was a stupid idea. The person I thought I recognised was not who I thought they were. But while we were sorting that out, this gentleman visited and said it would be a shame if I came all the way here, to Vancouver Island, and didn't see something of the place before I flew home. He offered to take me on a tour of the island by boat. I accepted. I'm sorry – I had no idea I had a tracker with me and I didn't intend to start a search. We stopped here for breakfast on the way back to Victoria. Am I in trouble?'

The male Mountie smiled. She'd got it right with him – the opportunity to patronise an incompetent woman tourist was too good to pass by. She wasn't sure she'd had the same effect on the woman, and it was the woman who now said, 'Would you like us to take you the rest of the journey by car? It would be no trouble.'

Mary was aware of the tension in the man beside her. She said, 'Thank you, but I wouldn't dream of it. I've had a marvellous time so far. Do you know, last night we parked – is that the right word when you're in a boat? – anyway, that's what we did. We parked close to a beach and just sat and watched. And we saw wolves! Chester has a zoo and they probably have wolves there, but these were real and they were wild.' She finished her bacon sandwich and looked at Max. 'Do you think we could get some more coffee?' Then she turned back to the Mounties. 'It's been an amazing adventure. Canada is a marvellous country. I made a mistake with the social media picture but I'm not sorry because, if I hadn't, I'd never have made this trip.'

The two Mounties looked at each other, and then the woman said, 'Well, if you're sure...'

'Really. I'm sure. But thanks for being so interested.'

The Mounties left, no doubt to file a report on the conversation they'd just had, but the world was not going to have to wait for that. The waitress and the short-order cook had listened to the whole exchange. Now the waitress, after serving more coffee, went back to the phone from which she had called the RCMP. This time, the number she looked up belonged to the newspaper's Port Hardy correspondent.

***

The reporter who had first run the story rang Claire. 'Mary Barnes is alive and well. She's been on a trip with a guy. I'm sure we can put two and two together – I imagine the long stay off the northern beach was so they could have sex under the stars. This guy's married, so he might be hearing from his wife in a little while. They are now in a boat heading south to Victoria. Boy, am I glad I didn't mention abduction. I'd have looked a complete idiot.'

Shortly after that, when this latest update was on television, Gene Cohen rang Miriam Donovan. 'Looks like you're in the clear. Max hasn't killed the woman – he's done a deal with her instead. Is that enough, or do you want *me* to take the woman out?'

Cohen could hear muted discussion at the other end. Then Miriam Donovan said, 'Leave her. It's a risk, but not as big a risk now as doing anything to shut her up. We're going to have to hope she goes on keeping her trap shut. And if she doesn't, there'll be the option of casting doubt on her mental health. But I'll be having a word with my brother about not putting his sister's interests first.'

***

Detective Sergeant Barney Fingleton wasn't having much success in finding another burglar who had been tapped up by Bob Barnes to enter the Unity Corp building illegally. He'd listed four possibles. Three had denied any knowledge of the proposed robbery in terms that had convinced Barney that they were telling the truth. And then there was Terry Findlay, who had laughed at him.

'Sergeant. Why on earth would anyone have asked me to burgle a building? What do I know about burglary?'

'How do you earn your living, Mr Findlay? How do you pay your mortgage and buy your groceries?'

'I'm a bricklayer. I don't have a mortgage. Like Lonnie Donegan's dustman father, I live in a council flat.'

'Oh, that's right. But from what I hear, you have a place in Gran Canaria. Quite the palace according to our sources. And another in Mallorca. And when did you last put one brick on top of another?'

'Your sources! I suggest you find some new ones – the ones you've got are obviously useless.'

'Have you ever heard of CRT?'

'What's that? Some kind of hormone therapy?'

'It stands for Civil Recovery and Tax. The National Crime Agency use it to get money back from people who make it from crime. And it's a civil law operation so it doesn't demand the same standard of proof as in a criminal court. We just have to persuade the court that on the balance of probabilities you obtained the assets you have by criminal means.'

'Yes, yes, but you still have to demonstrate that I own them. And you won't be able to do that. So roll it and tuck it, Sergeant.'

When he reported this to the next Major Investigation Team briefing, DCI McIntyre said, 'We'd never get the NCA interested in someone like Findlay. He's not big enough. But Holly Evans might be.'

***

Detective Sergeant Sally Fortune was having rather more success. She'd arranged for a drone to fly over Holly Evans's house in Ruthin. That had given her two car registration numbers: the Lexus convertible she already knew about and a black BMW. She'd put those registration numbers into the Automatic Number Plate Recognition network. Now she'd had a message that the BMW was heading south on a route that would eventually take it to the A5. She set off to join it. The A5 goes all the way from Holyhead to London, and she was going to have to call for help if it turned out to be on a long journey, but she was in luck. When the BMW reached the A5, instead of taking the eastbound direction that could take them all the way to London, it headed west. And not very far, because after about six miles it turned through the gates of one of the most prestigious and exclusive hotels in Wales. Sally counted ten seconds, then another ten seconds, and then she followed it in and parked some distance away.

Something was clearly going on here this weekend because the car park was full of high-end cars. Sally watched a solidly built man whose head was shaved to baldness get out of the BMW and walk a little way to where a man of about fifty sat in a red Ferrari. It looked as though he had chosen his spot in order not to be obvious, and it crossed Sally's mind that someone who did not want to stand out might have chosen a different car. The man with the shaven head chatted with the Ferrari driver through the Ferrari's open window. Then he walked back to his BMW and took from the boot a small case and an even smaller bag that Sally recognised as likely to contain make-up. He opened the BMW's passenger door and offered his hand. A young woman took it and stepped out. Then the man escorted the woman to the Ferrari, spoke a couple of words and went back to the BMW, which he drove out of the car park. Sally used her phone to photograph the Ferrari driver and the young woman walking into the hotel as though they had arrived together.

She was in very little doubt about what she had just witnessed. A little more information, though, was always going to be useful. She gave it ten minutes to allow the Ferrari driver and his escort to complete registration and reach their room, and then she went into the hotel. There was nothing so vulgar as a reception counter, but a well-dressed woman approached her. Sally produced her warrant card, taking care to be discreet. The woman said, 'Is something the matter?'

'No. I'm engaged on a routine enquiry. But I wonder if you would mind telling me what activities are taking place here this weekend?'

'May I just take a closer look at that ID you showed me?' When she had done so, she said, 'I'm sorry, I had to be sure you were who you appeared to be. I can count on your discretion?'

'Without question.'

'The hotel is given over to a wedding this weekend. Nothing else will happen here. The couple are socially important on a national scale and so are a number of their guests. I'd prefer not to be asked to name names.'

'Then I will not embarrass you. Thank you. You've been very helpful.'

* * *

'Socially important on a national scale!' said DCI McIntyre. 'My word – the airs some people give themselves. And a prossy among them.'

'I think she'd prefer "escort", ma'am,' said Sally. 'Or "call girl", at a pinch.'

'Well, whatever she wants to be called, she's going to get an even closer examination than this lecher with the Ferrari will give her. I want an unmarked car half a mile in each direction from the hotel exit, starting after breakfast tomorrow and going right through either till after lunch the next day or till the woman comes out. Tell North Wales Police what we're doing and say if they want to join in, they will be very welcome.'

'You can bet they won't.'

'I'm counting on it. Give the drivers the numbers of the Ferrari, the BMW and the Lexus. Do we know who owns the Ferrari?'

'Sir Henry Owen.'

'The industrialist? Bugger me. Okay, we don't want to upset him so if he leaves the hotel on his own, he is to be allowed to pass. We'll interview him later, and all we'll want to know is how he made the arrangements about the girl. But if he drives out with the girl, he'll have to be stopped. She comes out with anyone else, we stop them and we ask them to come here to answer questions. If they refuse, they are not to be arrested but we need identification. And find out who is doing the wedding photographs.'

The excitement Sally had been feeling took a sudden drop. 'Sorry, ma'am. I should have thought of that.'

'Don't beat yourself up. You did well.'

CHAPTER 26

Before they left the diner, Mary asked Max to buy her some cigarettes. When they got on the boat, Max said, 'My heart was in my mouth back there.'

'I could tell. I enjoyed it, if you want to know.'

'What decided you?'

Mary took her time over answering. 'It's difficult to explain. And yet it's easy. I'm a Fitzgibbon. If you knew the Chester Fitzgibbons, you'd understand just how difficult it would be for one of us to tell the police anything.'

'That was it?'

'That was most of it. And I decided I owed you something for coming back for me. Oh, look, I don't know. I had to make the decision, I had no time to think about it, so I did what my father always taught us to do. I lied to the police.'

'And when you get back to England? Will we still have a deal?'

'We'll still have a deal. But if I were you, I'd be worrying about the company my sister keeps.'

They were almost opposite the hotel when they saw the throng. Max said, 'Those are TV cameras. And press photographers, and where there are press photographers there are journalists. If you don't mind, I'll leave you here.'

'You don't want to take the credit for showing a poor tourist the island?'

'I'd rather fade into the background, if it's all the same to you.'

Max had been right; the place was full of reporters and they were all looking for her. There were two ways she could handle this – she could let herself be overwhelmed, or she could take charge. And Mary had never been very good at giving other people their way. She held up her hand. In a very loud voice, she said, 'Which one of you wrote that story in the paper? About me being lost somewhere?'

The reporter who had got the story from Claire held up her hand. 'That was me.'

'Come with me. The rest of you can bugger off.'

In her room, Mary went through the room-service menu. 'I'm going to have a club sandwich. And a beer. What's a good beer to drink in Canada?'

'Molson is Canadian.'

'Is that what you'd have?'

'Probably.'

'Then that's what I'll have.' She picked up the phone and waved the menu at the journalist. 'You want to join me?'

'Sure. I'll have what you're having.'

When she had ordered the sandwiches and the beer, Mary said, 'Sit down. Tell me where you got the story.'

'A woman called Claire Tanner came to see me. She wanted publicity for you. She said you'd been abducted, but that she'd put a pen in your purse and it had a tracker in it.'

Mary raised her eyebrows. 'The pen. That's how she did it. You didn't say anything in the paper about abduction.'

'I didn't want to take any risks. And after what you told the RCMP, I'm glad I didn't. I suppose you were telling the truth?'

Mary ignored the question. 'I lost my phone. So excited trying to take a photograph, I dropped it in the sea. Otherwise, I'd have called Claire Tanner.'

'You want to speak to her? Use my phone.'

'I don't, no. What I want is for you to give her a message after I've left this island. I also want you to help me get to Vancouver Airport without being chased all the way by people with cameras and microphones.'

'I can do that. In return for an exclusive interview.'

'So start interviewing.'

***

At eleven on Sunday morning, the hotel manager saw the arrival of a black BMW. A few minutes later, Sir Henry Owen escorted the woman he'd booked in with yesterday through the lobby and into the car park. When he came back he said, 'My wife needs to be in one place today, and I need to be in another.'

The manager smiled. 'It must be difficult having such busy schedules.' Did Owen sense the falseness of her sympathy? It didn't matter – the form of the thing had been observed.

* * *

She sat in the back seat, knowing that Laszlo preferred that. She passed two hundred and fifty pounds over the seatback to him. Harry had given her an extra two-fifty as a tip but that was hers to keep. That was the deal. Laszlo thanked her politely. He said, 'You okay?'

'Yes. Fine.'

'He didn't… Nothing out of the ordinary?'

She recognised what was coming. She'd been here before. 'You need me again today?'

'Is that possible? We've got an emergency – one of our young ladies has been rushed to hospital for an appendectomy. So, if you're available – and, as long as you're not, you know…'

His reluctance to say the words was cute when she considered the job he did and the sheer size of him. 'I'm not marked in any way, if that's what you mean. He's got loads of energy for someone his age but he doesn't want anything my grandmother would have objected to.'

'Your grandmother? Should we be auditioning her?'

She laughed. 'He's not a biter or a beater. And, yes, fine, I wasn't planning to do anything else tonight. I have a dissertation to submit but the due date isn't till Friday. Can you pick me up? And you'd better brief me on the client. What's this?'

'Looks like the cops to me.' He slowed down and pulled in to the side of the road. One police car had come up behind him, flashing the blue lights on the grill to get him to pull over; another had come straight toward them and was now parked right in front. When two uniformed officers approached the driver's door, Laszlo rolled down his window. 'Yes, officer. How can I help you?'

'Would you and the lady mind coming to Chester police station with us, sir?'

She stayed silent. She had committed no crime and she wasn't concerned but this could be a nuisance. Still, it was for Laszlo to deal with. He said, 'About what?'

'I understand that officers there would like to talk to you about money laundering, sir.'

'Money laundering? What would I know about money laundering?'

'CID don't share information like that with the likes of me, sir. We'd like the young lady to travel with us in my car, please.'

Laszlo said, 'Are you arresting us?'

'No, sir, nothing like that. It's just a chat. At this stage.'

Laszlo turned to look at her. She wasn't in any doubt about what the look meant. *You've been rehearsed for this. You know what to say and what not to say. Break a leg.* Then he turned back. 'Always cooperate with the police,' he said. 'That's what my mother used to hammer into me. Mind you, where I grew up, if you didn't cooperate with the police you might find yourself in an unmarked grave. That's why I came here.'

'Thank you, sir. One other thing…do you have any identification with you?'

Laszlo reached into a jacket pocket and took out a UK passport. 'As you can see, officer, I became a British citizen. No unmarked graves in this country. That's why I love it here.'

* * *

A little over an hour later, two police cars arrived at the station, together with Laszlo's black BMW. McIntyre said, 'You haven't arrested or cautioned them?'

'No, ma'am.'

'Excellent. Well done. We'll take it from here. Julie, you and Harry talk to the woman in interview room one. Barney and I will take the man. We'll be in interview room two. If either of them wants to leave, make no difficulty but we do need to have confirmed addresses. This is exploratory. I'm not expecting any charges to be laid today. Kid gloves, please.'

* * *

In interview room one, Nicola Walmsley said, 'Why have I been brought here?'

'I'll go through that in just a moment,' said Julie. 'First, I want to make a couple of things clear. You are not under arrest and you are charged with no offence. If you had been, you would have been brought into the custody suite, you would have been cautioned, you would have been given details of the offence about which you were being questioned and you would have been offered the services of a lawyer. None of those things has happened. This conversation is not being recorded and you are free to leave at any time. Now, would you mind telling me your name?'

'I'll tell you my name when you tell me why I have been brought here. And if that doesn't happen, then I'll test your honesty in saying that I'm free to leave.'

'Fair enough. We believe that it is possible that you have unwittingly become involved with people who have been engaged in money laundering. I stress that we are talking here about third parties. If money laundering has indeed taken place, no-one believes that you have had any part in it. Now, may I have your name?'

'I'm Nicola Walmsley.'

'Thank you. May I call you Nicola?'

'I suppose so.'

'Nicola, do you have any form of identification with you?'

'I have my driver's licence. Will that do?'

'Please.' Julie took the licence and photographed it with her tablet. 'And this address – is that where you live?'

'Yes, it is.'

Julie handed back the licence. 'Thank you. Would you mind telling me the name of the man who was driving you when you were stopped?'

'His name is Laszlo. I'm sorry I don't know his last name – I've heard it, but it's one of those unpronounceable things.'

'And what is your relationship with Laszlo?'

'Relationship? I haven't got one.'

'I mean, how do you know him? He came to the hotel this morning and collected you. How did that happen?'

'Oh, I see. That sort of relationship. Not a... No. Well. He's a friend. I can't remember how we met. At a party, I should think. But he became a friend. And I needed a lift this morning, so I rang him and he came for me.'

'Yes. I see. I believe it was also Laszlo who delivered you to the hotel yesterday afternoon.'

'Have you been watching me?'

'Not you, Nicola.'

'Laszlo, then. You're watching Laszlo. Why?'

'Nicola, have you given any money to Laszlo recently?'

'No. Why should I?'

'I understand you spent last night with a man. Would you mind giving me his name?'

'Yes. I would mind. In fact, I think it's time to bring this interview to an end.'

'As I told you, Nicola, you're free to leave at any time. And I don't like to think of this as an interview. It's more a conversation. I believe the name of the man you spent the night with is Sir Henry Owen?'

'If you know who he was, why did you ask?'

'I'm going to ask you another question now, Nicola, if you're prepared to stay here long enough to hear it.'

'Ask it. I don't promise to answer.'

'Before I ask the question, I'd like to make an observation. It concerns what is against the law in this country and what is not. And one of the things that are legal here is for a woman, provided that she is eighteen years or older and that no-one coerced her into it, to accept money from a man in return for having sex with him. And even if she was coerced, it would be the man who had sex with her who would be committing an offence and not her.' She let the silence run, but it was clear that Nicola was not going to comment. 'So there is no suggestion that I'm asking you to admit to anything illegal when I say that my question is, did you have sex last night with Sir Henry Owen and did he give you money in return?'

'That's actually two questions.'

'Yes, I suppose it is.'

'As it happens, I did have sex with Harry last night. He prefers Harry to Henry. At least among friends – I wouldn't suggest that you try it if you are foolish enough to start questioning him. And damn good sex it was. And, as it happens, he did give me some money. He knows I'm a graduate student, he knows I don't have a great deal to spend on myself, and he is a very generous man.'

'Thank you for being so open, Nicola. And did you give any of that money to Laszlo? Or to anyone associated with Laszlo?'

'No, I did not.'

'You do realise that, even if you had, you would not have been committing an offence? Even if it was Laszlo or someone associated with him who introduced you to Sir Henry, and even if the intention was always that you would have sex with Sir Henry in exchange for money and that you would give some of that money to Laszlo or someone associated with him, you would have committed no offence when you handed over that money.'

'No. I wouldn't. But he would. Wouldn't he? He'd have been acting as a pimp, and prostitution may not be against the law in this country, but being a pimp is. And Laszlo is not a pimp. He's just a friend. And now I am terminating this...this conversation, as you call it.' She stood up and left without another word.

When she'd gone, Harry Walford said, 'She didn't give us anything. Did she?'

'I'm afraid not. She's been well rehearsed and she has great self-confidence. Let's hope the DCI had a better result.'

But when they met later to discuss the two interviews, DCI McIntyre had nothing positive to report. 'He told me what she seems to have told you. Which was no doubt their intention.

He is a friend, he can't remember how they met but he thinks it was probably at a party, she rang to say she needed a lift, he'd been half expecting it because he did her a favour by taking her there yesterday, and he went to collect her. He says that's what you do for friends. She didn't give him any money and he says he wouldn't expect any. Nor did he give any to her. I'm afraid we're going to have to talk to Sir Henry Owen and see what he has to say. But I'll need to check that out at a higher level than chief inspector, or I may find myself back in uniform in a patrol car.'

CHAPTER 27

The interview over and the story filed, the journalist spoke to her editor and explained the deal she had made with Mary. The editor said she would call back. When she did, the journalist told Mary, 'Twenty minutes from now, we take the back stairs that are reserved for the staff. There'll be a car waiting to take both of us to Victoria Harbour. You'll take the seaplane to Vancouver Harbour. You'll be met there and driven to Vancouver Airport. As soon as you take off from Victoria Harbour, I'll go into the Fairmont Empress on the harbour where Claire Tanner is staying and give her your message.'

'I need to check out. And I need to do it in cash. What if the lobby is still full of reporters?'

The journalist picked up the phone and dialled Reception. 'Your guest Mary Barnes wants to check out but she doesn't want to do that in front of reporters and cameramen. Can you please send someone up here?' Then to Mary she said, 'That's arranged.'

Just under two hours after this conversation, the journalist told Claire that Mary was on her way home. Claire rang KLM, confirmed that she could be on a flight at 5.40 that afternoon, and she, too, checked out of her hotel. The receptionist said, 'Your room is paid for for another four days. If you give me your debit card, I'll credit your bank with the refund.'

Was it really only three days since she'd arrived here? She shook her head. 'It isn't my money. Please refund it to the people who paid it for me.'

Mary's message had been clear enough. 'I'm flying home tonight. If you get on the same flight, please don't talk to me until we are back in Chester. I don't want us to be seen together before then.' And so Claire was not able to tell Mary while they were travelling that she was now a widow. But she had kept Tina Howard aware of developments and before taking off she texted Tina with the flight's arrival details.

* * *

Late afternoon in Vancouver was early next morning in Amsterdam and it was noon when they landed there and mid-afternoon when they reached Manchester. Tina was at the airport with a photographer. Claire stayed close enough to hear Tina's opening words. 'Mrs Barnes, how does it feel to be returning to the home in which your husband was savagely murdered while you were away?'

A small part of Claire's mind could only admire the brutality with which the information had been delivered. A much larger part made her question whether she could ever have been a big enough shit to succeed as a journalist. She wrapped an arm round the stricken Mary to hold her up, but Tina eased herself between them. 'I've got a car waiting to get you back to Chester, Mrs Barnes.' To Claire she mouthed the words, *Not you*. 'The police have not yet released the Moor's Head, and so we've booked you into a suite at the Grosvenor.' She glanced in Claire's direction. 'The staff there have been advised that you need complete privacy during your stay. The only person other than hotel staff who will be admitted to see you is me.'

* * *

The first thing Claire did when she reached home was to ring Marie. 'Mary Barnes is safely back in Chester. Mr Fitzgibbon hired me to watch over her in Canada and keep her safe. I'm calling an end to the job. I'll send my invoice for incidentals in the morning.'

'I'll look after it as soon as it comes in.'

'Thank you.'

Then she called Daisy. 'I'm home. I'm also knackered. Give me three hours to nap and then come round. We'll order pizza. Can you bring wine?'

CHAPTER 28

'What are you going to do now?' said Daisy.

'I'm going to go back to work. My normal work, I mean. I've been to Canada, I've made more money than I've ever made for a week's work before, I've learned a few things… I don't think I covered myself in glory because I should have been there when Mary was abducted. But she survived. There's a question I'd like to ask the man who paid me all that money. Will I ask it? I haven't decided. But a private investigator's life isn't usually that exciting, and I'll be happy to settle for boredom for a while.'

'Do you ever hear from Winston?'

'I don't. And I'm not sure what I'd do now if I did.'

'If he wanted to get together again?'

'I can't say how I'd react. A while ago, I'd have jumped through hoops to get him back. But there's something about being rejected that makes me think "Okay, I accept your decision, but you'd better be certain it really is what you want because I'm changing the locks".'

'And have you? Changed the locks?'

'I rang a locksmith right after my nap. He'll be here in the morning.'

'Wow! You are serious. Our mother will be pleased.'

'Yes, well, pleasing her is not high on my list of things to do. And I don't suppose I'll tell her. Has she given you a hard time?'

'She knows Jayden's been arrested. It was in the paper. I told her we were through.'

'Well done. So here we are, two single women, eminently desirable and completely unattached. What we need is a holiday.'

'I'm game. Any idea where?'

'So long as it isn't Vancouver Island, pretty well anywhere will do me. As long as it has sunshine, a pool and a bar.'

'Ibiza?'

'Daisy, I don't think we're that young any more. How about one of the Greek islands? Meet some suntanned men?'

'I knew a woman who married a Greek. She didn't know if she was coming or going.'

'Daisy! I think you've been keeping bad company.'

'Sorry. Anyway, a Greek island sounds good to me. When shall we go?'

They spent the next hour googling holidays on Greek islands until the pizza was eaten, the wine was drunk and the flights had been booked. Then Claire said, 'Daisy, I'm bushed. I've done two fourteen-hour flights in four days with a lot of stress in the middle. Thanks for coming round. I'm so happy to have my sister back. Two weeks from now, we'll be sitting by the pool in Kefalonia. We'll drink

Greek wine and eat Greek food. And the only men we'll think about will be new ones.'

***

DCI McIntyre had told the superintendent who was her immediate boss that she wanted to talk to Sir Henry Owen. The Super had told her to wait while he cleared it with the Deputy Chief Constable. 'And I doubt that it will end there.' When the reply came, it was that no contact should be made with Sir Henry at DCI level. 'The Chief knows Sir Henry and he will speak to him.'

'Yes, sir. Am I allowed to ask what he'll say?'

'I think you can rely on the chief constable to get things right, Sylvie. It will be along the lines that we believe Sir Henry may have had contact with someone who may have been involved in money laundering. The chief will make it clear that he knows about Sir Henry's night with the Walmsley woman. That can be done on a man-to-man basis, which we have to accept that you would find difficult for purely biological reasons.'

'Yes, sir.'

'He will also make it clear that no judgement is intended. Sir Henry has been a widower for five years. Of course he needs the right kind of escort when he attends certain kinds of event. Naturally, they may be drawn to each other and certain activities may occur. That is a matter between Sir Henry and the escort. The only question the chief will seek an answer to is, did any money pass, in relation to Sir Henry's escort, that night to anyone other than the escort? And that, I believe, is the only answer you need.'

'Yes, sir.'

'Because, if Sir Henry paid money only to the escort and to no-one clsc, no-onc has committed any offence.'

'No, sir.'

'But if money was paid to someone else, then that person will have committed the offence of procuring or pimping.'

'Yes, sir.'

'But neither Sir Henry nor the escort will have committed any offence.'

'No, sir.'

* * *

The answer, when it came, was that Sir Henry had not been offended when the chief had asked the question over drinks at a function to which both had been invited, and that he had paid nothing to anyone, though he had given some money to the escort to help her with her life as a postgraduate student. 'So, as you see, Sylvie, neither Sir Henry nor the

Walmsley girl has anything to answer for. And the chief would prefer that Sir Henry hear no more about the matter.'

'Yes, sir. Thank you, sir.'

'So,' DCI McIntyre said to DI Julie Roberts later. 'We still have the unsolved murder of Bob Barnes and the attempted murder of Glenn Farrell to deal with. And we have got nowhere in finding the culprits. We have the DNA and the fingerprints of the people who stored drugs in the Unity Corp building and, if we can find them, we can question them in connection with the attack on Glenn Farrell. But when will that happen? And then we have the possibility that Bob Barnes was laundering money for Holly Evans. But to prove money laundering we have to show the money was the proceeds of crime. It's only money laundering if the person you were doing it for wasn't supposed to have it in the first place.'

'So we have to question Holly Evans.'

'Yes, we do. But before that, let's have a word with Mary Barnes and see what she knew about it. Get her in. No arrest at this point and no charges, and treat her with the kindness due to someone whose husband has been brutally murdered. But find out what she knew.'

* * *

The SOCOs had finished with the Moor's Head, and Mary had moved back in. It was fine for Sylvie McIntyre to say, 'Get her in,' but Mary was a woman who knew how the law operated and she didn't see the police as her friends. When a police car arrived and the driver offered to take her to the police station, she said, 'Am I under arrest?'

'No. I've just been asked...'

'Then I'm not going. Anyone who wants to talk to me can come and do it here.'

'Then go, Julie,' said DCI McIntyre when the constable reported Mary's refusal. 'And take Harry with you.'

* * *

Mary's first question, when they arrived, was, 'What do you want?'

'We'd like to ask about your husband's business.'

'The pub? The pub was his business. And mine, of course.'

'Well... Yes. But we'd like to know about any other business interests he might have had.'

'Like what?'

'Like money laundering.'

'Well, that's lovely. I have to say, I admire your cheek. Bob is just dead – slaughtered by somebody and as far as I can tell you haven't the first idea who that somebody was – and now you want to fit him up for something he didn't do. Got some money laundering cases going spare, have you? Looking for some mug to stick them to?'

'Mary...'

'Mrs Barnes, if you don't mind.'

'Mrs Barnes. No-one is trying to fit anyone up. We are simply trying to tie up loose ends. Does the name Holly Holdings mean anything to you?'

'Nothing. Should it?'

'How about Holly Evans?'

'Nope. Never heard of her.'

Harry Walford said, 'Laszlo?'

Mary shook her head. 'Foreigner, is he?'

'He's a British citizen, Mrs Barnes,' said Julie.

'Hm. Well, I never heard of him.'

'Every Monday for more than the last two years, this pub deposited a large amount of money in the bank.'

'Of course we did. The weekend's takings. Weekends are big business in a place as successful as this.'

'And every Friday, about ten thousand pounds was transferred to the account of Holly Holdings.'

'Ten thousand pounds?'

'Sometimes less, sometimes more. But always there or thereabouts.'

'Well. I wonder what that was about? You'd have to ask Bob. And, of course, you can't do that. I know nothing about it.'

'You do realise, Mrs Barnes, that if we are able to establish that those payments amounted to money laundering... And if we are able to show that you knew something about it...'

'Don't threaten me, copper. You do your establishing and then come back. And now you can go, please. You're not the kind of people I want my customers to see when I open those doors.'

'You're carrying on with the pub, then?'

'Why should I not? Bob and I made wills leaving everything to each other. That means I'm now the owner of the Moor's Head. Free and clear, if you'd like to know – there are no mortgages.'

'And have you had the licence transferred to you?'

'It's always been in my name. Bob used to be a bookmaker and for some reason the police objected to him having a licence. So I applied, and I have one. If you look over the door, you'll see my name up there. You can do that on your way out.'

Outside, Harry Walford said, 'Next stop Holly Evans?'

'First we have to update HOLMES about this visit. But, yes, I imagine a visit to Holly Evans will be assigned to us.'

CHAPTER 29

Claire was scrambling eggs for breakfast when her phone rang and the name Ted Hughes appeared on the screen. Scrambled eggs are an unforgiving dish if you leave them unattended, so she ignored the call and carried on stirring. When the eggs were spread out on hot buttered toast and she'd taken her first sip from a mug of tea, she pressed the button to return the call. 'Ted.'

'Thanks for calling back, Claire. I've had another call from the care home manager. Bert Musk is having one of his lucid days and he wants to see you. The manager says he's desperate for a meeting.'

'I'll go this morning. Shall I pick you up on the way?'

'Please. I'd hate not to be there.'

She wolfed her way through the scrambled eggs, finished her mug of tea and lippied up as she waited for the taxi to arrive. She told herself it was just another call on a possible witness. Something she'd done many times before. So why was her heart beating like this?

* * *

Musk looked as though every moment was a bonus and he could go at any time. The manager had found them a quiet room where they wouldn't be interrupted by other wandering patients. Claire put her phone on the table. 'I'm expecting a call, Bert, and I would have to take it.' But the button she pressed had started the Record app. 'You have something to tell me.'

Musk struggled to speak. Every sentence, even every word, was bought at the expense of fighting for breath. He said, 'I killed a woman.'

Claire didn't know how to respond.

'I cut off her head and the police thought she was someone she wasn't.'

The rapid beating of Claire's heart had slowed. Mary Barnes had brought her a mystery; she'd thought she would never get to the bottom of it and now it was almost here. She said, 'Sally Varney? Is that who the police thought it was?'

Musk had almost collapsed in coughing that Claire thought might carry him away before he said another word. Then, 'Yes. It was.'

'Why did the woman have to die?' Was it simple lust? Had she resisted Musk's advances and had he killed her for it?

'I was paid. Two hundred pounds, which was a lot at the time.'

'By...?' She needed all this on tape; if only Musk would tell his story a little faster.

'The money came from Sally Varney. And she was there when I killed the girl. She watched it all. But I think the money was Barry Fitzgibbon's.'

'Why do you think that?'

She could see that she'd irritated him. 'Will you just let me tell you what I want to tell you? Fitzgibbon knew I knew it was him. And Fitzgibbon would get someone to kill you for a lot less than thinking he'd murdered someone. So I let him know about the evidence I had.'

'Evidence?'

The effort it took him to reach into his pocket was written on his face. He produced a notebook and a piece of paper. He dropped them onto the table and Claire picked them up. He said, 'Fitzgibbon can't get me now. They've found me a place and I'll die there. Very soon. You do what you like with those.'

The piece of paper was a map. When he saw her looking at it, Musk managed a smile that made his face looked like a skull. 'It's a treasure map. We read *Treasure Island* at school when I was a kid. I never enjoyed reading much but I liked that book.'

'Treasure?'

'Not the *Treasure Island* sort of treasure. A different kind. The kind Barry Fitzgibbon would love to get his hands on. And wouldn't want anyone else to find.'

'And the book?'

'His customers. Not for cars. He was in the diamond business for a while. But he wouldn't want you to know that. He didn't like it when I found out.' He pulled down on the cord hanging by the wall. Then he pointed at what he had given her. 'Be careful with that. I used it to make sure I stayed alive. It could get you killed. Some posh spoken tart was here a few months ago offering me money for the book. She didn't mention Fitzgibbon, but her words could be? I told her I'd left it in a filing cabinet that went to a charity shop and when I went to get it back they told me they'd sold it to the people at Unity Corp.' The door opened and Rio Wood came in. Musk said, 'I need to sleep now. I'm very tired.'

* * *

Claire said, 'Let's go into town and have coffee.' Apart from that, they said nothing while they waited for the Uber and nothing during the journey. When they reached Marmalade on Northgate Street, they took a table as distant from any other patrons as possible. Ted looked at the menu. 'Eggy bread and bacon! That's for me. What are you having?'

'Just a flat white. I had breakfast before I came out.'

'So did I. But when will I get another chance for eggy bread and bacon?'

'It says here they're open seven days a week, Ted. Diamonds. What did you make of that?'

'Very interesting. Now we know how Barry Fitzgibbon made his pot.'

'We do?'

'I see the diamond scam is new to you. That should be a warning – if enough people don't remember it, it could make a comeback.'

'How did it work? Was he selling diamonds he didn't have?'

'Oh, he would have them all right. They just weren't worth what he told the buyers they were worth.'

'But he'd have been found out as soon as he delivered.'

'That was the touch of magic. People who ran the diamond scam didn't actually deliver the diamonds. What happened was, they'd tell the patsy they had these diamonds that were worth thousands. What they actually had were little industrial-grade diamonds, for use in drills and things, that were worth shillings, which is the currency we worked in in those days. But they'd say that these diamonds were being mounted with others in a piece of jewellery. A tiara, a brooch, a pendant – whatever you like. And the piece of jewellery would be rented out. Which is a legitimate business in the right hands. Honest hands. Someone going to a wedding, company dinner, old school reunion, they want to be seen wearing fancy pieces and they pay high prices to rent them for a few days. The scammer tells the mark the diamonds he's offering are going into jewellery that's already been rented to two, three, four people. And the mark will get ninety percent of all those rentals, and ninety percent of all the rentals that will follow. The rentals are so high, by the time ten people have rented the piece the mark will have doubled his money – and he'll still have the diamonds! What's not to like? He'd be a fool not to invest. And I say "he" because virtually everyone who fell for this scam was a man. I suppose women are not so stupid.'

'Or they don't have the discretionary spends men have, this world being what it is.'

'Or that. And the scammer pays the mark the money from the first couple of rentals, even though there haven't been any rentals. So now the mark knows the business is straight and if he has any more cash he invests that, too. There were people who lost their entire life savings. But by the time the rental money stopped coming in there was no trace of the scammer. And they'd never met him so they couldn't tell the police what he looked like. The accounts they paid money into had been closed and the people they were registered to didn't exist. The money had been taken out in cash so there was no audit trail to follow. The phones that had been used were discontinued – once again, customer names were false.'

'And this was big business?'

'The way I heard it, the number of firms operating the diamond scam was in double figures. I had no idea Barry Fitzgibbon was in onc of thcm.'

'Why would anyone invest that amount of money without seeing the person they were giving it to?'

'Remember I told you Barry had the gift of the gab? That's where it would have been useful. All of these sales were made on the phone. When Barry was younger, they used to say he could sell snow to Eskimos. Though these days I suppose you'd have to say Inuit. That would have come in handy in the car business, too. Show me that map.' When he'd looked at it, he said, 'The Berwyns. The same place as the body that was supposed to be Sally Varney's was burned. Do you know the area?'

Claire shook her head. 'I've driven through it, but I couldn't say I know it.'

'That just about describes the Berwyns. Wildly beautiful but a place people drive through. Maybe stop for a picnic but that's all.

They call them mountains but, really, they are big hills. And it's moorland. And bird sanctuaries. They have merlins there, which adds to the place's mystique. The idea of magic. I wonder what's there.'

'We need to find out.'

'Someone certainly needs to. But is it you? Or the police? Shouldn't you give them the map and the book? And the recording? Better still, give them to Tina Howard and let her get some more brownie points by being the one who hands them to the cops?'

'Yes. Of course I should.'

'But your face says you're not going to.'

'Oh, I'm sure I will. Eventually. After I know what's hidden in the Berwyns.'

'Do you mind if I come with you?'

'I'm counting on it. In case I get lost.'

'Shall we go now?'

'Here comes your eggy bread and bacon. Oh, and it has mushrooms, too. Have that and then we'll go.' She took out her phone. 'And I think I'll ask Dewi Morgan to come with us. He has a car, so he can drive us. And, no offence, but it would be good to have some muscle around the place.' When she'd finished the call she put the phone back on the table. 'Dewi can't make it till tomorrow. And whatever is there has waited thirty-two years, so I guess another day won't hurt. Are you enjoying that eggy bread?'

'It's delicious. Can't you tell?'

'I can, actually.'

'You don't have a car yourself? I stopped driving when I started worrying about my eyesight, but how do you manage without a car?'

'I have one. It's with the dealer, waiting for a new clutch.'

'I see. Listen, that recording on your phone is the only one there is. Isn't that a bit risky?'

'You want me to send you a copy? What would you do with it?'

'Nothing. Except keep it safe in case anything happens to yours.'

She thought about that and then she said, 'Okay. But I'm trusting you, Ted. I don't want to see this popping up as a story somewhere until I'm ready for that to happen. Now I'd better get back to the office. You'll be all right from here?'

'I'm old, Claire. That doesn't mean I'm incompetent.'

CHAPTER 30

It was Rio Wood's day off. He didn't normally do anything special because he couldn't normally afford to, so this time he planned to treat himself like a king, to eat all his meals in cafés and not in the room he rented and to buy something for himself that he would be able to look at for years and remember this red-letter day.

Of course, he was sad that poor Mr Musk was dead – but that was what happened. People didn't move into the care home and then go back out for a few more riotous years of high living. The care home was a departure lounge. Whatever came next – whether it was a blank and silent nothing or eternity in heaven or hell, whichever you had earned for yourself – that was where you were going next when you came to live here. And he had to say, Mr Musk had seemed a great deal calmer in his last few hours. Rio had no idea what had gone on in that last visit from the woman Claire Tanner and the man Ted Hughes, but, whatever it was, it had eased Mr Musk's anxieties.

He'd met Marie only once, when she'd identified him as the person most involved with Mr Musk's care. She made him a straightforward offer, which he had accepted. Mr Musk had a cousin, and Marie worked for him. He hated hospitals and care homes and anything that smelled of death. 'I know it's childish, Rio, but it's how he is. And even if he can't bring himself to visit, he wants to take responsibility for Mr Musk's funeral when the inevitable occurs. So, please – call me the moment Mr Musk dies. There'll be five hundred pounds in it for you. Cash, Rio, and in your hand – no need to trouble the tax man.'

If he was honest, he'd never believed in that five hundred pounds. It was too much. Too big a figure. But he wanted Mr Musk to have a decent funeral if that was at all possible. The care home always sent a couple of carers when a resident was buried or, more often, cremated and Rio had seen what a council-funded funeral was like. If a phone call would give Mr Musk something better, he would make that call. And he had. And Marie had come and talked to the manager. Then she'd talked to Rio as the carer closest to Mr Musk. He'd helped her collect all Mr Musk's personal possessions to take away and give to his cousin, though God knew there wasn't much. And, when no-one was around to see, she had slipped him ten fifty-pound notes. Rio hoped Mr Musk was now in heaven. Because that's certainly where Rio was.

***

As she'd expected, DI Julie Roberts was instructed to take DS Harry Walford to talk to Holly Evans. They were politely received and asked to wait 'while I attend to something I was doing when you arrived.'

Walford looked around him. 'I suppose this must be what people used to call a drawing room.'

'It's handsome, isn't it?'

'I wonder how she pays for it?'

'That's one of the things we are here to find out.'

A few minutes later, two things happened at the same time. One was that they saw Laszlo walk past the window toward where the cars were parked, accompanied by a young woman. The other was that Holly Evans came into the room, wheeling a trolley on which were a teapot, a coffee pot, cups and saucers, milk, cream and sugar, a bottle of sparkling water with glasses, and plates of biscuits and brownies. She poured a coffee, placed it on a small table beside an armchair on one side of an empty marble-surrounded fireplace and sat down. 'Please,' she said. 'It's much easier if you help yourselves than if I try to play hostess.'

Julie Roberts took coffee and a brownie and sat in the armchair opposite Holly Evans. Walford, who would need his hands free to take notes, helped himself to a glass of water.

DI Roberts said, 'You have a very attractive home. Do you live here alone?'

'Thank you. Yes, I do.'

'No servants?'

'A cleaner comes in once a week. I have a gardener. That's all. No maid, no cook. My parents had those things and I found them an imposition. I prefer to be free of that sort of thing.'

'Do you have a job?'

A slight smile touched the woman's lips. 'I don't. That's something else I prefer to be free of. I know idleness is disapproved of in these puritanical days, but I don't care about the opinion of other people.'

'Then would you mind telling me what you live on?'

'I think I just told you. My parents were rich. They lived in a country that no longer exists – Yugoslavia – and I preferred to get out of there when the new states that had formed out of the old one began to squabble. But I was able to bring my father's money with me. Well, not with me exactly – he had moved almost all of it to a bank in Switzerland and when he died I got the name on that account changed.' She smiled. 'I know that in Britain today that will be regarded as shameful idleness and indulgence, but there you are. I became a British citizen but I'm afraid I may not have taken on every single British idea.'

'You knew a man called Bob Barnes?'

Holly Evans's face was a perfect expression of innocence. 'Bob Barnes? I don't... No. I don't believe I ever heard that name.'

'He ran a pub in Chester called the Moor's Head.'

'Did he? I go into Chester occasionally – to shop, you know, and sometimes for lunch – but I never go into pubs. I don't know the one you're speaking about.'

'How very odd. Because, for quite some time now, Bob Barnes has paid money once every week into an account that was emptied a few days later and the money transferred to an account in the name of Holly Holdings with a bank in Hereford. The amounts were usually somewhere around ten thousand pounds. I believe Holly Holdings is your company.'

She watched with something approaching admiration as Holly Evans's face registered first astonishment and then dawning realisation. Holly said, 'So *that's* how it was done. I often wondered.'

'It?'

'The transfer. The money I mentioned my father transferring to Switzerland is only part of the story. I'm afraid I have to confess to being richer than that. There was a lot more in what used to be Yugoslavia, and the man who was my father's agent promised me that he would get it all to me. Of course I see the transfers coming in but I had no idea how he had managed it. Now I know – he does it through this man... What did you say his name was?'

'Bob Barnes.'

'Bob Barnes. The Moor's Head. I must go there and thank Bob for being the conduit.'

'I'm afraid that will be difficult,' said Julie. 'Bob Barnes is dead.'

'Dead! Oh, dear. Was he an old man?'

'No, I wouldn't call him old. He was murdered. Quite brutally.'

Holly Evans had covered her mouth with her hand. 'Murdered! Oh, that's dreadful.'

'Indeed. And particularly for him. He didn't transfer your money to you last week.'

'Didn't he? I hadn't noticed.'

'You didn't notice that ten thousand pounds didn't arrive in your account?'

'I don't monitor it every week, Inspector. I don't need to. The truth is, I have more money already than I'm going to need for the rest of my life. It might be shocking to admit that, but it's the way it is. If I ever got around to noticing that money didn't arrive one week I'd have assumed that my father's agent hadn't been able to send it.'

'Yes, I see. May we have your father's agent's name?'

The expression on Holly Evans's face now spoke of bottomless regret. 'Ah, now, Inspector, I'm sorry. You know, the country that used to be Yugoslavia is now a sad imitation of what it used to be. Life is cheap there. My father's agent has been very loyal. I couldn't expose him to the risk he would run if it was known there that the British police were making enquiries about him. I'm sorry.'

'That's a pity. You see, the theory that we are working on is that Bob Barnes was engaged in money laundering. And he was killed because he didn't deliver one payment. And the only money he appears to have been laundering was for you.'

'Ah, yes – money laundering. Laszlo told me you'd mentioned that. But I thought he'd satisfied your interest on that matter?'

'It was discussed with Laszlo, that's right. Though not by me. I spoke to a young lady called Nicola Walmsley. Do you know her?'

'Nicola Walmsley. No, Inspector, I'm afraid I can't help you there. The name means nothing to me.' She spread her hands out as if in sadness. 'I'm not being much help to you at all, am I?'

'But you do know Laszlo. May I ask how?'

'When other people ask that question, I tell them Laszlo is a friend. Since I'm now being asked by the police, I will admit the truth.

Laszlo is a bodyguard. He is there to make sure nothing happens to me.'

'Do you pay him?'

'I do. I pay him out of the money my father's agent transfers to me. That was part of the deal I made with my father's agent. I agreed to accept a bodyguard and he agreed to pay him.'

Now Harry Walford spoke for the first time. 'He's your bodyguard – but he doesn't live here?'

'He has a room in one of the hotels in town. That suits both of us – he doesn't have to bother about keeping the place clean, he gets his laundry done, and English pub food suits him better than what I like to cook. If I need him in a hurry, he can be here in minutes. And, let's be honest, he has a number of girlfriends. In fact, he was here with one of them when you arrived.'

'Could we have her name?'

'You could if I knew it. I'm afraid I don't even try to keep track.' She had finished her second cup of coffee by this time and now she looked at her watch. 'Is there anything else? Only I have some correspondence to deal with.'

'One more thing before we go,' said Julie. 'You said you were brought up in what used to be Yugoslavia. I take it Holly Evans is a name you assumed when you came here?'

'That's right. Would you like to know the name my parents gave me? Let me write it down for you – you might have trouble with the spelling.' She turned to Walford. 'Give me that tablet you're making notes on.'

When she'd done that, the two detectives stood up. Julie said, 'Thanks for being so open with us.'

'Always help the police,' said Holly as she led them to the door.

When they were back in the car, Walford said, 'Thanks for being so open! I don't think she told us a single true thing.'

'No. Clever, isn't she? She won't crack under interview. We're going to need some very solid forensics before we can tie her to the murder of Bob Barnes. We'd also need to prove beyond doubt that the money Bob Barnes paid into her account every week actually came from her.'

'Do you think she knows who killed him?'

'No. As it happens, I don't. I think she's managing a string of girls and that's where the money comes from, but I think she's too clever to get involved with murdering a publican. And there's no way that girl we saw was Laszlo's girlfriend. He was delivering her to a client.'

'She had a quite ethereal beauty,' said Walford.

'Put her out of your mind. Ethereal or not, she's right out of your price bracket. You'd need a freebie. And I'd bet anything you like she doesn't give those.'

CHAPTER 31

Next morning, Claire carried her coffee and muffin into her office and placed them on the desk. She unlocked the door into the yard and stepped outside, holding her cigarettes and a lighter, but she didn't get to smoke because two men who should not have been there picked her up and carried her back into the office. She reached into her bag for the pepper spray but one of the men said, 'Don't be silly,' and took it from her. 'You have to come with us.'

'I'm damned if I will.'

'Well, darling, you're dead if you don't.'

Why hadn't she had an alarm fitted to this building? She knew the answer – she never kept anything of value here – but if there had been a button to press... Well, there wasn't. The man who hadn't spoken yet had gone. She looked at the man who'd been doing the talking and saw a knife in his hand. He said, 'Guns make a noise. If you're going to carry one of these,' and he waved the knife in her direction, 'you have to know how to use it.' He paused, like an actor, for a single beat. 'And I do. Here are my instructions. If at all possible, I have to get you to come quietly and I have to make sure you bring your handbag and any other bags with you. If you make that impossible, I have to take the bags with me. I also have to search your pockets. But before I do that, I'll cut your throat. I hate seeing that amount of blood, especially when it isn't necessary and all the man wants to do is ask you a couple of questions and check whether you have something belonging to him. Then he'll let you go. So, really, live or die, it's your choice. And the good news is, you get to make it now.' He gestured toward the door, and Claire saw that a four-by-four had driven up outside. 'Shall we go?'

She had a choice. Jimmy Ojukwe was now only prepared to put her in the ring with men because she was a match for them. These two didn't know that and, if she added the advantage of surprise to being at such close quarters, she could probably take the pair of them. But that ignored the knife. He might be lying when he said she'd be free to leave when she'd answered some questions, and he might be lying when he said he'd kill her if she refused to get into the car, but how could she be sure? She only had to look at his face to know he meant it. And if she went along with this kidnapping she might learn something she needed to know. As she moved toward the door she said, 'And who is the man?'

'You'll find that out when we get there.' He took her phone and handbag from her and picked up the laptop bag. 'Is this all there is?'

Dewi Morgan rang Claire to ask what time she wanted to be picked up. There was no answer. He rang again after ten minutes, and then ten minutes after that. Still no answer. He drove to her office and found both the street door and the door to the backyard unlocked, but no-one around. He called her once more and, when she continued not to answer, he rang Ted Hughes. 'Is Claire Tanner with you?'

'Haven't seen her since yesterday.'

'I'm at her office. It's the Mary Celeste here – all the doors are open, the lights are on, but no-one's in. A bit like a Man U player.'

'City supporter, are you?'

'And she doesn't answer her phone. She said you both wanted to go down to the Berwyns today.'

'That's right. She has a map we want to investigate.'

'A map? We need her with us, then.'

'Ideally. But I've seen the map. I know the Berwyns, I can get us to the area.'

'Is there any point in going without her?'

'She may be in trouble.'

'That's a risk of the job she does.'

'I mean trouble related to having that map.'

'Sounds like you know more of the story than I do.'

'Come over to my place. I've got a tape you should listen to.'

Claire sat in the back of the car and the man with the knife sat beside her. She said, 'Where are we going?'

'You'll find out.'

They headed north on Liverpool Road toward Chester Zoo and then joined the bypass but, when they reached Backford, they turned off to the left. Station Road, it said, but if there had ever been a railway here it was long gone. A few well-kept houses, a sign offering Cheshire potatoes and then they were on a country road only just wide enough for two vehicles to pass. A right turn, another left and then they were heading south on Long Lane and Claire knew what was going on. They'd taken this roundabout route to avoid being seen. They'd kept her out of the centre of Chester in case she was later reported missing and someone told the police they'd seen her with two men whose own mothers would probably describe them as thuggish. Now Queensferry was ahead of them and the large Deeside Industrial Estate was to their right, but they weren't going to pass through either. These people knew the land around here, they knew where they were going, and they were going to make her disappear. The man beside her had put his knife away but he still had it. Trying for the casual approach, she reached out a hand and tried the door handle, though where she'd go if she escaped the car out here and how she'd avoid recapture she had no idea. The handle did nothing and the man beside her smiled. 'Childproof locks, darling. You'll get out when we say you'll get out.'

A little more manoeuvring on roads with names but no numbers and they were pulling into a farmyard. Someone stepped away from the hedge and closed the gate behind them while the car drove into a large barn that was empty except for a tractor, two folding chairs and a card table. The man who had closed the gate followed them in and closed the barn door behind him as the driver opened Claire's door and motioned her out. She turned to look at the newcomer. It was Barry Fitzgibbon. Without looking at her, he sat down on one of the folding chairs. The man with the knife put Claire's two bags on the table and Fitzgibbon emptied them, carefully and one after the other, onto the table.

He picked up the map and the book that Bert Musk had given her. Then he looked at her for the first time. 'These are mine. I think you know that. Were you planning to bring them to me?' When she didn't answer, he said, 'Did you have some other plan? It does matter, Claire. I want you to think about your position for a moment. No-one knows you're here. Not many people know this farm belongs to me – registration of the ownership is quite complicated. We don't have visitors. We could dig a nice rectangular hole, six feet long and six feet deep. We've done it before. We wouldn't even need to kill you first – put you in the hole, cover you with soil and let nature take its course. Is that what you want?'

Claire stared at him. She was the boxer and mixed martial arts fighter, but there were three of them. Still, she wasn't going to show fear. Fitzgibbon was a bully. When bullies thought you were scared, they stepped up the bullying.

'Or, of course, now that I have what belongs to me, we could drive you back to Chester and let you go. That would be the easy option. Probably my preferred choice. As long as you haven't copied any of these documents.'

And there it was – she had kept the fear off her face and the bully had backed down. Her father had taught her that when she was in primary school and being bullied by others bigger than her. 'Never show your fear,' he had said. 'Bullies feed on fear. It's like roast chicken with all the trimmings. They can't get enough of it.' And then of course there was the time she was fifteen and abducted for the pleasure of a man she'd never met. That was why she'd got into the MMA and the boxing – to make sure she never had to submit to someone else's will again.

Fitzgibbon was looking straight at her. 'So have you?'

'Have I what?' Those were the first words she'd spoken since she'd been put into the car outside her office.

With an expression of exaggerated patience, Fitzgibbon said, 'Have you copied this map? Have you copied any of the entries in this book?'

'No. I haven't.'

'Good. But we'll just have a look, shall we?' He opened her laptop and pressed the On button. 'I hope this is charged. What's your password?' When she didn't answer he said, 'If you don't tell me, we'll dig that hole I mentioned and put the laptop in it with you. So let's try again. If you don't want to tell me your password, you can keep it secret.' He turned the laptop in her direction and pushed it across the table. There was nothing to gain from refusing. She typed her password, hit the Enter key, and pushed the laptop back toward him. He started browsing File Explorer. 'No – I can't see anything on here. Mind you, this looks interesting.' He had opened one of her client files. 'Charlie Mathers – I know him. We meet at functions. Charity fundraisers, that sort of thing. So he thinks his finance director is milking the company? Interesting.' He went on reading and then his face lit up. 'And you found out the finance director is shagging Charlie's wife! Poor old Charlie.' He looked at the other two men. 'See? Marriage is not a good idea. Women will cheat you.' He picked up the map. 'That's what this is all about, really. Though we don't need to get into that. Okay, I think we're done. Take her back to Chester. Drop her right where you picked her up.' He looked at Claire. 'No harm done. Thanks for looking after my sister. And thanks for bringing this book to me. I've worried about it for more than thirty years, and now I need worry no longer. If I have any more jobs I need a private investigator for, you will be top of my list. Enjoy the rest of your day.'

How to deal with bullies was not the only lesson Claire's father had attempted to teach her. Another was not to be precipitous. To think before she spoke. He'd been less successful with this one and now, instead of going to where the car door was already being held open for her, she said, 'How did you come to know Eugene Cohen?'

'Excuse me?'

'Eugene Cohen is a Canadian private investigator who started out in Ontario and now lives in British Columbia. So he isn't someone you would be expected to know in the normal course of events. But he has been to Chester. He came thirty-two years ago. He was hired to mislead the parents of a

Canadian girl who disappeared here. Her name was Ellen Hubbick. When your brother Jim was jailed for murdering Sally Varney, I'd lay odds that the person who died wasn't Sally Varney at all. It was Ellen Hubbick. Somebody must have paid Eugene Cohen a handsome sum of money to cover the murderer's tracks. And I don't suppose many people in Chester have ever heard of Eugene Cohen. But you have, because you sent him to get in my way. And paid him, too.'

She knew she'd made a mistake. If eyes had ever been as cold as Fitzgibbon's were now, Claire had never seen them. Yet still she went on. 'Why did Ellen Hubbick have to die, Barry? And how did Sally Varney get involved?'

'She involved herself. She got into a relationship with my brother Jim because she couldn't accept that what she really wanted was another woman. When she met Ellen Hubbick, she couldn't deny her feelings any longer. Jim found out and wanted to kill the pair of them. He got as far as Ellen – Sally found out and ran for her life.'

'That isn't what Bert Musk said.'

'Bert Musk is dead, so he isn't going to be giving evidence.' He turned away from her. 'Either of you two know how to work that digger?' When they looked blankly at each other, he said, 'It can't be that difficult. Well away from the house, please. Six feet deep, six feet long, two feet wide. You got any cable ties?'

'There's a box of them in the car.'

'Tie her to the tractor till the hole is dug.' He turned back to Claire. 'You disappoint me. It's true Eugene Cohen did a job for me. And so did you. Cohen was well paid for what he did. And so were you. And Cohen kept his trap shut. Which is where the similarity with you disappears. As you are about to.' To the two men he said, 'I'm going to follow this map. When the job is done, give me a call. I promise you'll be happy with the reward.'

'Hold on a minute. You want us to kill this woman? We have no problem with her.'

'But I do.'

'Then you kill her. Or, if you want us to do it, you pay us.' He looked for a moment at his colleague. 'One thousand pounds. Each.'

'Okay. Come and see me in my office tomorrow.'

'No, no – that's not how it works. You pay us now. Or there'll be no killing.'

'How the hell am I supposed to do that? I don't carry that kind of money in cash.'

'No problem. I've got a debit card with my bank details on it.' He looked again at his colleague. 'Have you got yours with you?' When the man nodded, he went on, 'So you use whatever method you contact the bank by, and you pay each of us a thousand pounds. Then you can go, and we'll do your job for you. Otherwise, no deal.'

* * *

When Fitzgibbon had left, the man who'd done all the talking looked at Claire. 'What's this about? Why does he want you dead?'

She felt like asking *Weren't you listening?* but for once her father's advice took hold. 'Because I found out he paid someone to kill a woman thirty-two years ago. And he's afraid of what I might do with the information.'

'He got away with it?'

'*He* did. His brother has spent the last thirty-two years in prison for the murder. And his brother had nothing to do with it.'

The man turned to his colleague. 'You hear that? Fitzgibbon paid someone to murder a woman and then dumped the murder on someone else. And now he wants to pay us to murder another woman. How many people have you killed?'

'Me? None. You know that. Roughed a few up, sure. Hurt one or two badly, I admit it. But killed? No.'

'Me neither. You want to start now?'

'So what do we do?'

They were looking at her again. The one with the knife said, 'Kidnap is a serious crime.

If you tell the cops we brought you here by force, we could get some heavy time.'

If ever there was a time for compromise, this was it. 'I won't say a word.'

'You mean that?'

The other one said, 'What choice do you think we have? We're not going to dig a hole and put her in it. We know that and so does she. We have to trust her.'

Claire said, 'No offence but I have bigger fish to fry. I want Barry Fitzgibbon and Sally Varney jailed for conspiracy to murder. Nothing else matters to me.'

This time, she sat alone in the back of the car while the two thugs sat up front. Before they closed her door they had switched the childproof lock off. With her phone back, she rang Dewi.

'Claire! Where the hell are you?'

'It's a long story. I'm on my way to the office right now. Should be there in about forty minutes.'

'Can you come to Ted Hughes's house instead?'

'Yes, I think so. I'll ask my driver to drop me there.'

CHAPTER 32

After trying three times without success to reach Claire by phone, Tina Howard rang Ted Hughes. 'Do you know where Claire Tanner is?'

'No. I know where she's supposed to be, which is with me and Dewi Morgan on our way to the Berwyns to check out a map. But she's disappeared. Why are you looking for her?'

'I had some information I thought she might like to know.'

'Well, *I've* got some information *you* might like to know. It's on a tape which I'm going to play to Dewi as soon as he gets here. Why don't you come over and you can listen to it, too.'

When she got there, Ted said, 'What was the information you had for Claire?'

'When she brought Mary Barnes back from Canada, you know we put Mary into a hotel for a couple of days and I got her to do a brain dump? If you can call what Mary Barnes has a brain? Well, I haven't been able to use that yet for fear of "doing a Claire" and upsetting the cops, but it did inspire me to make some enquiries. One of which was, what was Ellen Donovan's maiden name?'

'Ellen Donovan?'

'The woman Mary Barnes thought was Sally Varney. She married Miriam Donovan in a civil ceremony and took the Donovan name. But I wanted to know what she'd been called before that. I was hoping it would turn out she'd been called Varney.'

'And had she?'

'No. The name on the certificate is Ellen Hubbick. And we had a visit a few days ago from Ellen Hubbick's father and sister. They want to find her so they can be reconciled before her mother dies. I'm trying to get hold of the Hubbicks to tell them where their daughter is, but I thought Claire would like to know, too. Why are you looking so grim?'

'If I were you, I'd hold off contacting the Hubbicks till you've heard this tape.'

* * *

Two hours later, Dewi Morgan turned off what passed for a road deep in the south-west corner of the Berwyn Mountains and on to a track that looked as though it was only ever used by sheep. 'You sure this is what the map said? I'm glad I've got a four-by-four. I wonder what that BMW is doing by the side of the road.'

'That's Barry Fitzgibbon's car,' said Claire. 'Or if it isn't, it's very like.'

'That's good,' said Morgan. 'Whatever is here, we'll catch him with it. Tina, this could be the biggest story you ever had. You should have brought a camera.'

'I've got my smartphone. God, this is an isolated place. I had no idea there was anything like this so close to home. And I'm glad we haven't had to walk this far on this terrain, the way it looks like Fitzgibbon has.'

Fitzgibbon had taken the map from Claire and so, although they had found the general area, if he had not still been there they would never have found the cave. But there it was, and there was a very tired Barry Fitzgibbon holding a black plastic bag that looked even more past it than he did. Morgan led the way, while Tina stood back and took photographs. Fitzgibbon was staring at Claire. 'What are you doing here? Why aren't you dead?'

Morgan said, 'I'll take that, Barry.'

'You will not. It's mine.'

'Barry. We can do this the hard way if that's what you want. But let's be honest with each other. When you want violence done, you hire other people to do it. When other people want violence done, they hire me. Now be sensible and give me the bag.' But when he reached out to take it, Fitzgibbon swung it away from him and thirty-two years took their toll on plastic that had only ever been meant for temporary use. The bag split and something fell on the ground and rolled a little way before stopping. Tina had moved forward and was snapping away as fast as she could.

'My God,' said Hughes. 'It's a skull.'

Claire said, 'Is that what Bert Musk used to keep you away from him? The threat that you'd be exposed as Ellen Hubbick's killer?'

Fitzgibbon said, 'Bert Musk killed Ellen Hubbick. Not me.'

'But you paid him.'

'I'd like to see anyone try to prove that.'

Tina Howard was speaking on her phone. 'Police, please.'

Fitzgibbon said, 'What the hell is she doing?'

'I expect she's calling the police,' said Claire. 'That's the usual practice if you find human body parts lying around the place.'

Without another word, Fitzgibbon rushed past them and started down the track back to his car. 'It's all right,' said Tina. 'I've got him and the skull in the same pictures. He won't be able to deny he was here. The police want our location. Anyone got an app to give me the coordinates?' After she'd passed them on she said, 'They're on their way. We are to wait here but not to touch anything. Apparently, they'll be regarding this as a crime scene.'

CHAPTER 33

A few days later, DCI Sylvia McIntyre called the team together. 'Major Investigations has no interest in the discovery of a thirty-two-year-old skull unless it can be connected to the murder of Bob Barnes and the attempted murder of Glenn Farrell. And I don't think it can. So we leave it to CID. Nancy Hubbick gave a sample of DNA close enough to the DNA extracted from the teeth in the skull to identify it as belonging to a sibling of hers, which means it belongs to Ellen Hubbick. That's a matter for CID to deal with.'

DS Barney Fingleton said, 'We do know that Bert Musk murdered Ellen Hubbick at the instigation of Barry Fitzgibbon.'

'Do we, though, Barney? How do we know that?'

'We have the tape. Musk confessed.'

Sylvie said, 'But how do we know that, Barney? Was that tape recorded in accordance with the Police and Criminal Evidence Act? Of course it wasn't. Is there anything, other than the word of the retired reporter and the private eye who recorded it, to confirm that the voice actually belongs to Bert Musk? No, there isn't. It isn't up to me, it's up to whoever investigates that case, but if I were in charge there's no way I would present that tape to the Crown Prosecution

Service and ask them to charge Barry Fitzgibbon. They'd laugh at us. Any barrister worth his salt would get a jury doing the same thing. The tape is interesting, but without a confession from Fitzgibbon it's worthless. And he knows that, and he actually did laugh at us. No, we have nothing on Fitzgibbon. CID have passed a transcript of the tape to Jim Fitzgibbon's lawyer and I understand that he is going to seek to have Jim Fitzgibbon's conviction set aside as unsafe.'

Harry Walford said, 'What about Sally Varney?'

'We know nothing about Sally Varney.'

'But, surely – she's the woman passing herself off as Ellen Donovan.'

'Yes, I'm sure she is. But can we prove that?'

'We could compare her DNA with Tom Fitzgibbon's. That would tell us whether she was his mother.'

'And to get that, we'd need an extradition warrant to bring her here from Canada. To get an extradition warrant, we'd have to charge her. To charge her, we'd have to persuade the CPS that there was enough evidence to mount a prima facie case that she really is Sally Varney. And I happen to know that CID have already discussed that informally with the CPS and been told to forget it. The Canadian police have been told what we have and they will be asking the woman calling herself Ellen Donovan how she came into possession of Ellen Hubbick's passport, and why she passed herself off as Ellen Hubbick at the time of her marriage. But that in itself is not an offence that would enable us to get her extradited.'

Fingleton sighed. 'It must have been a lot easier in the old days when they didn't have to bother about PACE and the CPS.'

'Yes, Barney, I'm sure it was a great deal easier when it was us who decided whether to charge someone and all we needed to get a confession was to beat the shit out of them or keep them awake for seventy-two hours till they coughed to something they hadn't done. But that's why we now have PACE and the CPS. Because they may have been rotten apples, but too many coppers showed they couldn't be trusted. We wouldn't have known any of this without Claire Tanner. But Claire Tanner is a private investigator. She can ask any questions she likes in any way she likes. She can get to the truth, and this time she has. But no court is going to place any value on what she tells them, because she hasn't gone about her enquiries the way the law says she must. That's the difference between a private investigator and us. And if we don't follow PACE, the courts won't listen to us, either.

'So back to our cases. Bob Barnes and Glenn Farrell. I've talked about this to the Super and we've agreed that it's time to scale back the investigation. Until whoever left their DNA and fingerprints in the Unity Corp building leaves them somewhere else and we find them, we're not going to make progress. So the cases remain open, but I'm standing the whole team down.'

Julie Roberts said, 'What about Holly Evans?'

'What about her? Are you seriously suggesting the Major Investigation Team should spend time investigating a business that connects men wanting a shag with women wanting to be shagged? Why stop there? Why not go on and try to close down all the online dating agencies? Neither Holly Evans nor anyone connected with her has been shown to have committed an offence. We think she has – we think she's acted as a pimp – but we are miles away from proving that. Before this case blew up and you were drafted into this team, you all had a full caseload. You passed it on to colleagues to look after for you. Go, now, and take the cases back. I have no doubt we'll all be meeting again sometime soon, because that's the level of serious crime conducted in this neck of the woods. Until then, be about your normal business.'

Holly Evans was onboarding another new girl. They'd reached the point where she talked about money. She said, 'It used to be easier than it is now. We agreed the fee with the client but he paid you. Then you gave Laszlo half the money when he picked you up. But business is booming, and large amounts of cash are becoming ever more difficult. So now we send you a bill for limousine services and you pay us online. You can manage that, can't you? Only pay us half of the agreed fee – the rest is yours. And clients usually tip the girl when it's all over and all of that tip is yours to keep. You should never hear from the police, but if by chance you do and they want to know what the limousine services involved, you tell them that you were going somewhere with a friend, you were likely to drink alcohol and so you couldn't drive yourself, but the location required more than a simple taxi and you knew us to be a high-end limo service The police will know exactly what you were up to, but bear in mind that you are not breaking any laws. We'll rehearse from time to time to keep it fresh in your mind. Now Laszlo will run you home. I'm expecting to call on your services tomorrow, so get plenty of rest this evening. Never forget you are playing the part of an older man's dream, and older men like their dreams to be fresh, sweet-tempered and full of energy.'

When Laszlo returned, he said, 'This limousine business. Won't you have to pay tax?'

'That's all right. I don't mind paying tax. This country has been good to me.'

'You never feel like going home?'

She shuddered. 'For what? To see my mother, worn out before her time and still living in a hovel? Or my father, who started abusing me when I was twelve and trading me to men when I was fourteen? No, Laszlo. I like it here. The occasional trip to Nice, Madrid or Monte Carlo – fine. Back home? Never.'

'Didn't you tell those coppers that your father was a wealthy man who left you a pile of money?'

'Coppers! You wouldn't have used that word when you first got here. This country's been good to you, too. Yes, I did tell them that. And they have no way of making contact with anyone back there who can tell them differently.'

***

Ten days after the discovery of the skull, Claire and Daisy were sitting by the pool at a hotel in Kefalonia. Daisy said, 'That woman you went to Canada to ride shotgun for.'

'Mary Barnes.'

'What happened to her? I mean, really happened?'

'You've read Tina Howard's story?'

'Yes, but that didn't tell me much. It felt like she was watching her back.' Claire didn't say anything; her sister knew all about how her own carelessness about what she could say and what she couldn't had ended her journalistic career. After a pause, Daisy said, 'So what did happen?'

'Well, not what Mary Barnes wants us to believe, I'm pretty sure of that. But I couldn't prove it without her help, and it doesn't matter now anyway.' She sipped her drink and looked around. Then, 'Although,' she said, 'if we knew what had happened, I think we'd feel better about the world.'

'Because...?'

'I think that guy took her out on the water intending that she wouldn't come out alive. And then something happened to change his mind. He thought better of it.'

'I suppose that's something to be grateful for.'

'Yeah. It doesn't always look like it, but slowly the world is becoming a better place. People who would once have killed are slower now to do it. People who would once have lashed out are gradually becoming people prepared to talk. We should be glad.'

Daisy nodded. 'What about the guy who paid you to go? What about that skull?'

'Oh, the skull. Well, that doesn't show humanity in such a good light. I think that skull shows that Barry Fitzgibbon paid for the murder of Ellen Hubbick. He did it because she had a book – an account book – a list of records that would show how he'd conned people out of huge sums of money. He wanted it back and he was prepared to kill for it. But he didn't get it back, because the man who was paid to do the killing didn't trust him so he kept the book as collateral. What I find really appalling is that Barry Fitzgibbon paid for that murder and then let his brother spend more than thirty years in jail for it.'

'Unforgivable.'

'Yes. But there are people prepared to behave like that.'

'In spite of which, you think the world is becoming a better place?'

'Yes. I do. But we still have a way to go.'

Daisy was looking away from the pool toward the bar. 'Those two guys look interested.'

'So let them make their move. That's their job, not ours. Just concentrate on looking cool.' Claire peered at the two men over the top of her piña colada.

'Looking cool? That's what you think you're doing, is it?'

'I'm giving it my best shot.'

'Did you let Winston know you'd be here?'

'No. There'd be no point. He rang me.'

'Yes?'

'He read Tina's story, too. It mentioned my name. He rang to say I shouldn't be going to risky places. Or so he said. But really he was calling to let me know he's with someone else.'

'How do you feel about that?'

'I'm over him. You have to be, don't you? Even if you're not.'

'Yes, I'm afraid you do. Heads down – I think those two guys are about to head this way.'

And at that point, Claire's phone rang. 'Claire? I hope you're enjoying your holiday?'

'I am, thank you. Nice of you to think of me.'

'Well, it wasn't quite that simple.'

'No, I didn't suppose it was.'

'When are you back?'

'Who wants to know?'

'A potential client.'

'A potential story for you, you mean. I hope it's nothing like the last one you brought me.'

'That's very ungrateful, Claire. As I recall, the last one I brought you earned you more money than you'd ever made for a single job. Would you like to hear about this new one?'

Claire looked up. The two men who had been looking at them were now standing two feet away and close enough to be already in conversation with Daisy. She said, 'Will it wait till tomorrow?' And she put the phone down without waiting for an answer. 'Daisy. Who are these charming men? Please. Introduce me.'

Author's Note

I hope you enjoyed this book; I'm hard at work on the next in the series. You may like to know about the Batterton Police Series, which I write in the same name:
Drawn to Murder
Death to Order
Murder under Surveillance

Here are my books under other names:

Sharon Wright: Butterfly
No-one gives Sharon a chance – except Sharon. A crime novel set in gritty South London and rural France. Sharon woos the way a female mantis might – knowing that, when she's done, the male may have to die.

Darkness Comes
Ted Bailey stares Death in the face. And Death blinks first. Ted Bailey has got away with drug dealing, gunrunning, and even murder. Now he faces the ultimate judge. A death sentence, surely? But all is not as it seems.

Zappa's Mam's a Slapper
Born into the family from hell. Destined for a life of crime. In prison at 14. But Billy's life is not over yet. A coming-of-age story that begins

in tragedy and ends in hope. A bittersweet story of love, loss and one young man's refusal to accept what life offers.

The James Blakiston Series

A Just and Upright Man and *Poor Law* (with more to come)

Set in the north-east of England in the 1760s, the James Blakiston Series is historical fiction from the point of view of people at the bottom of the social heap and not the top.

Printed in Great Britain
by Amazon